Suddenly, Elizabeth saw herself standing on the shore of Secca Lake in the brittle sunshine. A girl glided toward her in slow motion—a girl who might have been Jessica, except for a cold, hard look in her bright blue eyes. The girl pulled off her hat, and shoulder-length dark hair tumbled out. She whipped out a butcher knife, and . . .

Elizabeth shook her head to clear it of the memory. It was the recurring nightmare she'd had for weeks after the accident.

SWEET VALLEY High®

BEWARE THE BABY-SITTER

Written by
Kate William

Created by
FRANCINE PASCAL

BANTAM BOOKS
NEW YORK · TORONTO · LONDON · SYDNEY · AUCKLAND

RL 6, age 12 and up

BEWARE THE BABY-SITTER

A Bantam Book / November 1993

Sweet Valley High® is a registered trademark of Francine Pascal
Conceived by Francine Pascal
Produced by Daniel Weiss Associates, Inc.
33 West 17th Street
New York, NY 10011
Cover art by Joe Danisi

ISBN: 0-553-29856-9

Published simultaneously in the United States and Canada

Bantam Books are published by Bantam Books, a division of Bantam
Doubleday Dell Publishing Group, Inc. Its trademark, consisting of the
words "Bantam Books" and the portrayal of a rooster, is Registered in
U.S. Patent and Trademark Office and in other countries. Marca
Registrada. Bantam Books, 1540 Broadway, New York, New York 10036.

PRINTED IN THE UNITED STATES OF AMERICA

OPM   0 9 8 7 6 5 4

Chapter 1

Enid Rollins lay on her stomach on a beach blanket and watched as her best friend, Elizabeth Wakefield, emerged, dripping, from the surf.

Elizabeth waved as she began strolling up the beach toward Enid. The warm, California sunlight sparkled on her wet shoulders, casting a small shadow on the sand at her feet. Her new blue maillot looked great—sexy, but in an understated way.

Enid sighed, only a little bit enviously. Mostly, she was just happy that things were finally beginning to work out for her friend. Elizabeth had been through so much in the last few weeks—ever since the night of the accident in which Sam Woodruff had been killed.

1

Most people in Sweet Valley—even Elizabeth's own twin sister—had initially held Elizabeth responsible for the accident. Elizabeth herself still couldn't remember much of what happened that night. The police said she had been driving the Jeep home from the school's Jungle Prom, with her sister's boyfriend in the seat beside her. Sam had died instantly in the crash, and both teenagers' blood-alcohol levels had measured well above the legal limit.

Thankfully, Elizabeth had been cleared of involuntary manslaughter—but only after the driver of another car had come forward during the trial and admitted that the accident had been his fault. The mystery that remained was the question of how Elizabeth had gotten drunk in the first place. Enid knew her best friend pretty well. Elizabeth Wakefield, the most responsible member of Sweet Valley High's junior class, did not drink—let alone drink and drive.

Enid raised herself on one arm and cupped her chin in her hand. Maybe they would never know what had really happened that night. But it was wonderful to see Elizabeth looking happy and normal again.

"I honestly don't know what to do about

Elizabeth," Jessica said, playing listlessly with her avocado-and-tomato sandwich. It was just after noon on Saturday, and she and her new boyfriend, James, sat on a blanket in a picnic area in the mountains, an hour outside of Sweet Valley.

James touched her hand sympathetically. "Have you tried talking to her?" he asked.

"Of course I've tried—well, sort of. I just don't know where to begin. And I'm not sure Elizabeth wants to talk to me."

"What were things like between you and Elizabeth before all this happened?"

"Things were wonderful," Jessica said. She leaned back on the picnic blanket and stared at the treetops. "Elizabeth and I have always been more than sisters, James—we've been each other's closest friends."

"So you always got along perfectly?"

Jessica laughed. "Not exactly," she admitted. "In fact, we were at each other's throats half the time! But we've always, *always* been there for each other. It's funny. We look so much alike that our brother calls us Clone One and Clone Two. But as soon as we open our mouths, we're about as different as two people can be."

"How are you different?" asked James, handing her an apple fritter.

Jessica shook her head. "You are the sweetest guy in the world to let me talk your head off like this. But you can't possibly be interested in hearing me babble on for hours about myself—"

James gently took her face in his hands. Beneath his longish light-brown hair, his eyes were as blue as the California sky. Every time Jessica looked into them, she felt a thrill.

"I can't think of anyone I'd rather hear about than you, Jessica," he said quietly. "In fact, I want to know everything about you—and I want to help you patch things up with your sister, if that's what *you* want. I can't bear to see you unhappy."

Jessica felt something inside her melting as James reached out with one hand to wipe the tear that had begun to roll down her face. *He's too good to be true,* she thought. *I don't deserve him after what I did to—after what happened to poor Sam.*

"It was Elizabeth's fault!" she said suddenly, her turquoise eyes blazing. "It doesn't matter where she got the alcohol. She shouldn't have been with *my* boyfriend in the first place!" She stopped as James put a hand on her shoulder. "I'm sorry, James," she murmured. "I'm *sorry.*"

"It's OK, Jessica," James reassured her. "You don't have to be ashamed of being angry. You know you can tell me anything."

"You're so nice. I don't deserve it."

"You deserve to be treated like a queen," said James. "I hate to see you so upset. You'll feel better if you talk about it. Tell me about Elizabeth. You say that the two of you have nothing in common—except that you're the two most gorgeous girls in California. How are you different?"

"Elizabeth has always been the perfect one— quiet and smart. She's just the opposite of me. She's on the honor roll, her room's spotless, she's never been late to anything in her life, and she never gets into trouble—"

"Until recently," James interjected.

Jessica nodded solemnly. "That's for sure," she said. "I think Liz has always been a little boring, really. *I'm* the one who knows how to have fun—I'm always the life of the party!" She sighed. "But not so much, these days."

"I can't think of anyone who would be better company," James said simply. He leaned forward and kissed her gently on the lips.

Jessica smiled at him for a moment before continuing. "Lately, I hardly know myself," Jessica said. "I'm not used to being so scared and unsure."

"You never have to be scared when I'm

around, Jessica," James said, beginning to clear away the paper plates and napkins. "But now I've got a cure that's guaranteed to make you feel better."

"You already have made me feel better," Jessica told him. "You've taken me out here to the mountains where everything is so pretty. You packed a gourmet lunch. And you're putting up with me blabbing on like this. What could be next?"

"Next, I take you up there," he said, pointing through the treetops to a rocky outcrop on a nearby peak. "We're going hiking."

"All right," she agreed. "I warn you—I've never been the outdoorsy type—unless you count sunbathing. But I'd follow you any-where."

"Life is great!" exclaimed Elizabeth, smoothing back her wet hair as she plopped down on the beach blanket next to Enid, her blue-green eyes twinkling.

"Speaking of great, so is that new bathing suit I helped you pick out!" Enid said, turning onto her side to get a better look at her friend. "You look fantastic! You're lucky to have a best friend with such marvelous taste in clothes."

"I'm lucky to have you for a best friend, period," Elizabeth declared. "Really, Enid, I don't know how I'd have made it through the last few weeks without you."

"Oh, I'm sure you would have muddled along somehow," said Enid, pushing her unruly, reddish-brown hair out of her eyes.

"No, I wouldn't have," Elizabeth said. She shook her head so firmly that her golden blond hair—darker now that it was wet—flew out around her face, sprinkling Enid with sparkling drops of salt water. "And now, Enid, the ordeal is over, it's a beautiful Saturday, and I feel like a new person!"

Enid raised her eyebrows. "I'm surprised to hear that from you so soon," she said. "Glad, but surprised."

"You're going to hear it a lot from now on," Elizabeth vowed.

"Well, you certainly look wonderful," Enid said. "Every guy on the beach is probably scoping you out right now."

Elizabeth bit her lip, thinking for a moment of Todd Wilkins, her boyfriend. Then she shook her head. *Make that ex-boyfriend.*

Enid touched her arm. "Todd?" she asked.

"Yeah," Elizabeth admitted with an uncertain smile. "You always know exactly what I'm worrying about, Enid. You know, I really thought there was a chance at Lila's parents' wedding. When I danced that one dance with Todd, for a few minutes everything was perfect again. I thought he felt it too, but I guess I was wrong. He didn't *say* anything. He hasn't tried to talk to me at all." She shrugged. "Well, I can't hang on to that relationship any longer. It's over with Todd. I've finally faced the facts."

Enid smiled sympathetically. "Are you sure?" she asked. "You two were so much in love."

Elizabeth nodded. "Yes," she said decisively. "Now that I've got my self-respect back, I refuse to lose it over a guy—even if it is Todd." She rolled her eyes. "At least he isn't going out with my *sister* anymore!"

Enid nodded. "Jessica and Todd did seem like an odd match-up," she admitted. "I'm sure she was only dating him to get back at you, but I don't know what motivated *him*."

"Me neither," Elizabeth admitted. "But it doesn't matter now. Jessica just started dating that dirt-bike racer, James, and already seems head over heels in love. I'm really glad for her, Enid. Jessica's been through so much."

She reached for a towel. "Of course, I wish things were patched up between Jessica and me. I don't think we'll ever be really close again, but at least Jessica has stopped acting like she hates me. Now I'm going to get on with my life. I can do it—even without Jessica."

"And without Todd?" Enid asked.

"Without Todd."

Elizabeth smiled mischievously, wrapped the towel around her wet head, and began furiously rubbing at her hair. "I'm gonna wash that man right out of my hair!" she sang, realizing as she did that it was the kind of outburst people would expect not from her but from her more outgoing sister.

Enid laughed. "Speaking of men, Hugh has to go to his cousin's bachelor party on the night of Olivia Davidson's costume ball. How about if we two single girls go together?"

"It's a date!" Elizabeth said. "In fact, I can't wait. It sounds like it's going to be a wonderful party. Olivia's new boyfriend, Harry, seems like a lot of fun. She said the whole party was his idea."

"He does have a flair for the dramatic!" Enid agreed. "Olivia's lucky. No guy has ever wanted to meet me enough to make up a phony arts foundation and invite me to speak at it—just to get me to come to his house!" She reached for the suntan lotion. "But what about Winston Egbert?" she asked jokingly. "After all, he was your date for the Fowler wedding. Will I be breaking his heart if I go with you to the costume party?"

9

Elizabeth placed the back of her hand against her forehead in mock despair. "It's all over between Winston and me," she said dramatically. "His girlfriend Maria Santelli got back to town the day after the wedding, and that was the end of our torrid affair."

Enid laughed. "I never thought of you as the boyfriend-stealing type."

"Seriously, Winston's been a good friend through all of this," Elizabeth said. "I should think of some way to thank him for sticking by me."

"Oh, I don't think Winston needs much of anything this week!" Enid said.

"I forgot," Elizabeth admitted. "He's been bragging to everyone about the wild and crazy time he's going to have with his parents out of town—"

"Oh my gosh . . ." Enid interrupted in a whisper. She was staring intently at something—or someone—down the beach.

Elizabeth followed her gaze. "What is it?"

Enid blinked her eyes. "She's gone now," she said slowly, still staring.

"Who?"

"It was the weirdest thing, Liz," Enid said. "There was a girl down the beach a few hundred yards away, and she looked like she was staring straight at us. It really gave me the creeps. Maybe the sun's playing tricks on my eyes, but I could've sworn it was Jessica—or *you*—except that she had dark hair. It was uncanny!"

Suddenly, Elizabeth saw herself standing on the shore of Secca Lake in the brittle sunshine. A girl glided toward her in slow motion—a girl who might have been Jessica, except for a cold, hard look in her bright-blue eyes. The girl pulled off her hat, and shoulder-length dark hair tumbled out. She whipped out a butcher knife, and . . .

Elizabeth shook her head to clear it of the memory. It was the recurring nightmare she'd had for weeks after the accident.

She forced a laugh. "You're imagining things, Enid! Jessica's miles away from here. James took her for a picnic in the mountains. And this town sure isn't big enough for *three* Wakefield twins! It must be sunstroke. You've been out in the sun too long!"

Enid nodded, but Elizabeth saw her glancing nervously down the beach.

The noontime sun was warm, but Elizabeth shivered.

After an hour of hiking, Jessica peered over a low stone wall. Directly below the rock ledge where she and James were standing, a craggy ravine carved a deep gash in the rugged landscape.

"The view from up here is incredible!" she exclaimed. "I had no idea we were this high!"

"It's one of my favorite places," James agreed. "And you know, this is the first time I've really wanted to share it with someone. Nobody else has ever been special enough to bring to such a special place."

Jessica smiled warmly at him, and then gazed out again over the edge of the steep cliff. "This rock ledge juts out so far that I can't even see the wall of the cliff below us," she said. "It almost feels like we're flying!"

Sunlight reflected off the rocky ledge where Jessica stood. She shielded her eyes from the glare and peered into the murky depths, where the afternoon sun couldn't penetrate the steep banks. The narrow ravine was torn by dark, jagged boulders and punctuated here and there by solitary pine trees.

Jessica shuddered. She turned, embarrassed, to see if James had noticed her irrational fear, but he was staring into the ravine.

Suddenly, he grabbed her arm. "Look at that, Jessica!" he whispered, pointing over the wall to a spot almost directly below their rock ledge. "Do you see it?"

Jessica leaned over the stone wall and stared into the ravine. "Do I see what?"

"There's a deer down there," James said. "It's a fawn, standing right by that big pine tree."

"I don't see any deer," Jessica said, climbing onto the stone wall. "Are you sure you're not making it up?"

"No, honest!" James insisted. "It's *way* down there. Look closer to the side of the cliff."

"I still can't see it," Jessica complained. "It's not fair. You're taller than me."

She inched her body along the width of the wall to look out over to the very edge of the out-cropping. Then she leaned over the edge and peered into the dark ravine. "Now I really feel like I'm flying," she said, with an uncertain laugh. "But I still don't see the deer. Are you sure it's still there?"

"Oh, it's there, all right," said James. "But don't lean out so far—it's not safe."

Jessica was about to agree, but then she thought she saw something move in the darkness below. She extended her body as far off the edge of the wall as she dared, and peered deeper into the gully.

The black, spindly pine trees stood up like needles among the sharp boulders. The only movement Jessica could see was in the trees themselves, rising up like stalagmites to meet the ends of Jessica's sunlit hair. The trees tilted. The ravine whirled below Jessica as she felt James's hand on her back. She cried out and groped for the edge of the stone wall.

Then Jessica was sitting back from the edge of the wall, clutching it with both hands. She stared wide-eyed at James, remembering the feel of his hand on her back as the jagged boulders and black trees tilted wildly beneath her. Suddenly, she wanted to run right past him and scramble down the trail.

"You almost fell," he said quietly. "I had to grab you."

Jessica shook her head. She stared wordlessly at James, breathing heavily. Then she climbed off the wall and walked past him—away from the ravine.

"You're white as a ghost," James said. His blue eyes were full of concern as he stepped forward and took her in his arms. "But I would never have let you fall. You know that, don't you?"

Jessica buried her face in his shoulder. "I *know* you wouldn't," she whispered. But she couldn't forget the pressure of his hand on her back as the dark trees swayed beneath her.

Chapter 2

"Free at last!" Winston Egbert exclaimed loudly to the empty house. "It's Sunday noon, the parental units are visiting Aunt Sarah for an entire week, and I am *totally free!*"

Winston pulled a jar of peanut butter from the kitchen cupboard, waltzed to the counter with it, and began making his favorite sandwich.

"This is incredibly awesome," he said aloud. "No parents around to be grossed out by a perfectly good peanut-butter-and-sardine sandwich!"

He put the finishing touches on his creation and was about to pull out a chair at the kitchen table.

"The kitchen table?" he asked himself. "What am I thinking? House rules are off! I can eat in

15

the living room, if I want to—in front of the television set. And I don't even have to take a napkin!"

He sauntered into the living room, jumped onto the white couch, and put his tennis shoes on the glass-topped coffee table. "Ah," he sighed. "This is the life. This is going to be a truly radical week!"

Winston took an enormous bite of the sandwich. As he reached for the television remote control, he heard a knock at the door.

"Cmmmggh!" he yelled, his mouth full of peanut butter and sardines. He jumped up from the couch, ran to the door, and opened it, still chewing.

"It's Winston, right?" asked the harried young woman at the door. In one arm, she held a plastic tote bag with a dorky-looking design of dancing hippopotamuses. In the other, she cradled a soft bundle, wrapped in a light-green blanket.

Winston nodded, chewing furiously. He recognized the plump, dark-haired woman as Betsy something-or-other. She had moved into the neighborhood a few weeks earlier.

"Winston, I've got a tremendous favor to ask you," she said quickly. "You know me, don't you? I'm Betsy Zvonchenko. I just moved here from Wisconsin. My husband and I are renting the

Morgans' house, around the corner—you know, the little yellow one with the brown trim—since Dave and Caroline Morgan are on sabbatical for a year."

Winston gulped down the mouthful of sandwich and opened his mouth to reply, but Mrs. Zvonchenko was too fast for him.

"I know this is a terrible imposition," she said. "But I don't know another soul in California, and your mother has been kind enough to drop by with some groceries and to invite us over for dinner last weekend—even though, of course, we did turn down her offer. But we're new here and haven't had time to make any real friends, and I couldn't think of anyone else to ask, so I thought that your dear mother might be willing to—"

"Actually," Winston interrupted, "she's out—"

"I'm so sorry I missed her," the woman continued. "But I really can't wait—my plane's leaving in an hour, and I'm already late."

Winston opened his mouth again, but Mrs. Zvonchenko rushed on.

"You see, my husband's a journalist in Central America, and there's been one of those coups, you know, when they take over the government? Ian's fine, thank goodness, but he can't leave the country because his hotel was taken over by terrorists and his passport was in his room. He was

17

downstairs in the restaurant at the time and was able to get out, but now he's stuck in customs and they won't let him leave the country—"

"I'm terribly sorry," said Winston. "I wish there was something I—"

"Aren't you sweet?" Mrs. Zvonchenko interrupted. "I knew you would say that. That's why I thought I'd come over here. You know, I said to myself, 'Betsy,' I said, 'that nice Mrs. Egbert and her wonderful family might be kind enough to watch little Daisy overnight, while I travel to Central America to bring Ian his birth certificate so those ridiculous customs officials will let him leave the country.'"

Her tongue should be arrested for speeding, Winston thought. As she continued breathlessly, he shrugged his shoulders and took another bite of his sandwich. Sooner or later, she'd have to come up for air.

"Ian's in no danger, of course," Mrs. Zvonchenko was saying. "But communication out of such places is so limited at times like this. There's no other way for me to get the birth certificate to him but to bring it down myself. Of course, I can't take an eight-month-old child into such a situation, you understand—even if there is no real danger. Besides, you know how cranky babies get on long flights—"

Winston opened his mouth to reply.

"I'm talking too quickly, aren't I, Winston?" Mrs. Zvonchenko said, cutting him off again. "Ian calls me Turbo Tongue! He says nobody can ever get a word in edgewise."

Winston's eyes widened as wailing sounds began emanating from the green-blanketed bundle Mrs. Zvonchenko was carrying. *This is definitely out of my league,* he told himself.

Mrs. Zvonchenko was undaunted. "It must be time for Daisy's bottle," she said brightly, struggling to see her watch around the edge of the soft bundle. Then she shrugged her shoulders and held out the baby. "Here," she said. "You take her while I find her pacifier. It'll have to do for now."

Before Winston knew what was happening, he was holding the warm, squirming thing. Mrs. Zvonchenko's conversation didn't slow down at all as she rooted through the tote bag.

"Thank you so much, Winston, for agreeing to do this. It's such a load off my mind. Daisy won't give you much trouble. She's a very good baby. She can't exactly crawl yet, but she's just figured out how to creep along, and she can really get up some speed when she wants to, so she does take some watching. I'll be back tomorrow night—"

19

"But I don't know anything about—" Winston managed to say.

"That's perfectly all right, dear," said Mrs. Zvonchenko, reaching forward to place the plastic pacifier in the baby's mouth. "Until your darling mother gets home, just give Daisy her bottle. There's nothing to it. And remember to keep her little bottom dry!"

She leaned forward to set the tote bag on the floor. "The bag contains plenty of diapers," she said, "and some cans of formula, a few clothes, and Daisy's favorite giraffe. Oh, and she likes it when you sing to her."

"But I—" began Winston.

"Good-bye, little Daisy!" Mrs. Zvonchenko said, leaning forward to kiss the baby on the forehead. "Now, I must be going, or I'll miss my plane! Tell your mother how much I appreciate this, Winston. I'll see you tomorrow night."

Winston opened his mouth to object, but was too dazed to utter a sound as Mrs. Zvonchenko raced down the front walk.

The pacifier fell from Daisy's mouth and the baby began to wail indignantly. Winston's mouth was open, too, but couldn't make a sound. He jiggled the screaming baby in his arms as her mother disappeared around the corner. In one hand, he still held the half-eaten peanut-butter-and-sardine sandwich.

Sunday afternoon, James lay on the bed in his one-room apartment, cradling the phone with his chin.

He spoke again into the receiver. "Elizabeth is the responsible one, Mandy—"

"Huh?" said the girl on the other end of the line. "Oh," she added quickly. "Go on, James."

James narrowed his eyes and wondered for about the sixteenth time how much this Mandy girl was keeping from him—*if Mandy was her real name.* He was beginning to have his doubts about that, even. She always seemed startled when he used it.

He shrugged. She could call herself Jack the Ripper, for all he cared. Two thousand bucks was two thousand bucks.

"Elizabeth gets good grades," he continued. "She's the person everyone at school tells their troubles to. Jessica's always been more of a partier. But since her old boyfriend died, she's been more serious—more like her sister."

"What about hobbies?" Margo asked intently. "Does Elizabeth have any?"

"She wants to be a writer," said James. "She works for the school newspaper, and she likes to read."

"That's not very much to go on," Margo said sharply. "I'm not sure you're earning your pay. I hired you to go out with Jessica because I need to know *everything* there is to know about the Wakefield twins—especially Elizabeth. *And I mean everything!*"

James shuddered at the sinister note he heard in her voice. *This Mandy is one weird chick.* But he could deal with her, he told himself with a grin. And dating a gorgeous blonde wasn't exactly combat duty.

James still didn't know why Mandy wanted all this information on the Wakefield family, but he'd handled enough of these kinds of jobs to know not to ask too many questions. She hadn't asked him to do anything dangerous, or illegal— not yet, anyway. All in all, it looked like this was going to be the easiest two thousand dollars he'd ever earned.

"Don't worry, Mandy," James reassured her. "Jessica is like putty in my hands. Remember what I told you about what happened yesterday on the mountain. I was trying to see if she trusts me completely. And she does. She really thinks I was trying to save her. But I could've *killed* her if I wanted to."

"Let's leave that to the experts," Margo said.

James's eyes widened as he wondered again:

Just who is this girl, and what is she after?

"What about the twins' relationship?" Margo asked, sounding perfectly ordinary again. "Has it warmed up any?"

"It's hard to say. They're still not speaking much, but Jessica doesn't seem so hostile. She still resents Elizabeth for Sam's death, but she acts as if she feels kind of guilty about it herself—"

"That doesn't make sense," Margo interrupted, exasperated. "Jessica Wakefield doesn't strike me as having enough backbone to kill anybody."

"Heck, no," James said, shaking his head. "Jessica's a sweet kid. I didn't mean she had anything to do with Sam's accident. Maybe she argued with him that night, and never got a chance to tell him she was sorry. That kind of thing would bother her."

"Yeah, that sounds about right," said Margo. "But what's this 'sweet kid' stuff? You're not starting to like her, are you? Remember whose two grand you're working for, James. I can be very tough on employees who get their priorities mixed up."

James fumed inwardly. *Who does she think she is? Nobody threatens me and gets away with it.* He opened his mouth to reply, but then shut it, remembering the money.

"Don't worry, Mandy," he said after a moment. "Jessica's not my type. I like women who are more . . . *experienced*. Jessica's just a blond, blue-eyed two-thousand-dollar bill"—he couldn't help smiling broadly—"with great legs."

"Yeah, yeah," said Margo. "But while your eyes are on her legs, I want you to keep your *ears* on what she's saying."

"Anything in particular?"

"Find out more about the night Sam kicked," Margo ordered. Her tone was commanding, but James held his tongue.

"Nobody in town seems to know what was going on with the twins that night," she continued. "I hear Elizabeth was a total freak—not the usual Miss Goody-Two-Shoes act. And nobody's sure why she was with her sister's boyfriend. I want all the dirt. And if Jessica does have something to feel guilty about, I want to know what it is."

"I'll get it for you," James assured her. "But I'd better get it fast. Another few dates with *me*, and Jessica won't even remember Sam's name!"

"What else have you found out about the parents?" she asked suddenly.

"Jessica thinks they're great," James replied.

"She also thinks that Elizabeth's their favorite, but she's a little paranoid about that. They sound like the usual, boring, respectable suburban parents."

Margo's voice took on a quiet, dreamy quality. "Isn't Alice Wakefield the most beautiful, perfect mother?" she asked. "She's warm, loving, and protective."

James noticed a fervent, almost obsessive tone in her voice.

"She would do anything for her daughters— anything at all," Margo continued. "She always keeps them near her. She doesn't let other people hurt them or criticize them." She raised her voice an octave. "Isn't that right, James? Isn't that what Jessica says about her mother?"

James realized his heart was pounding. *This girl is beginning to seem more and more flipped out.* He shook his head in disgust.

"Yeah, Mandy," he agreed, telling her what she obviously wanted to hear. "Jessica likes her mother a lot. In fact, until lately, the whole family was like one of those television sitcoms—perfect parents, perfect kids, perfect house." He rolled his eyes.

"Good, very good," Margo said in a distracted voice. "Keep getting close to Jessica. Find out everything you can."

"I will. I've got another date with her Tuesday night."

"It's time to start the next phase," Margo said suddenly.

"What next phase?" asked James.

Margo went on as though she hadn't heard him.

"I've chosen a day-care center," she said. "The one run by Project Youth. It's called Little Darlings Day Care, and it's pretty close to Calico Drive. It'll be a good place to learn more about the people in Sweet Valley . . . because kids talk. And I have ways of getting them to talk to me."

James had no idea what she was talking about, but there was something seriously wrong with this girl. Maybe this wasn't such an easy way to earn two thousand dollars, after all.

"Jessica, do you have a minute?" asked Alice Wakefield, walking into the dining room that night.

"Sure, Mom," said Jessica. She looked up from the book that lay open on the table in front of her. "I might as well take a break. I'm certainly not getting anywhere with this algebra assignment."

Alice tried to hide her amused smile, but

Jessica was pretty sure she knew what her mother was thinking.

"I know, Mom," she admitted. "It's Sunday night, and I should have started my homework two days ago. And if I studied every day, like Liz, instead of once every leap year, I might understand the difference between the x-coordinate and the y-coordinate, and that—"

"Whoa, Jess!" her mother said, laughing. She pulled out the chair next to Jessica's and sat down. "I didn't come in here to criticize your study habits."

"No?" said Jessica, surprised. "You mean I wasted all that humility for no reason?"

"I promise I'll forget every word. You can use it all again the next time I *do* criticize your study habits."

Jessica pushed her algebra book out of the way. "So what did you want to talk to me about?"

Alice hesitated. "Did you have a good time hiking with James yesterday? You seemed a little upset when you got home."

"Oh, that was nothing," Jessica said. "I leaned too far over the edge of the mountain and almost fell off. But James caught me in plenty of time."

Jessica spoke flippantly, but she couldn't help remembering the chasm tilting wildly beneath her and the feeling of James's hand against her back. . . .

"Jessica," her mother said, interrupting her thoughts. "I don't want you to take this the wrong way. But your father and I are concerned. You've been through a terrible time, and we don't want to see you hurt again. We know so little about James. For one thing, he's a bit older—"

"He's eighteen!" Jessica protested. "Just two years ahead of me."

"And he doesn't go to school."

"He graduated last year. Not everybody can afford to go to college right away. But I'm sure he will eventually, if he can save up some money—"

"Jessica, all I'm trying to say is that I want you to take it slowly. You're still vulnerable right now. Even a boy who cares about you might take advantage of that without meaning to hurt you."

"I know, Mom," she said, suddenly understanding her mother's drift. "And I promise to take things slowly. But don't worry—James has always been a perfect gentleman."

"Good. I was hoping you wouldn't think I was being a nagging mother." She pulled Jessica's algebra book forward and pantomimed rolling up her sleeves. "Now let's take a look at these x- and y-coordinates of yours. I studied algebra myself a few hundred years ago."

Margo had another one of her headaches that night. It felt like an ax handle pounding against her forehead—pounding, pounding, pounding. She'd been having these headaches for some time now—ever since she started hearing the voices that spoke only to her.

"No!" she yelled, eyes squeezed shut as she stood in front of the rickety dresser in her tiny room at the boardinghouse.

"Think of nice things," Margo ordered herself aloud. She forced open her newly blue-green eyes—the same shade as the Wakefield twins' now, thanks to the colored contact lenses she'd bought at the mall. She looked at herself in the cracked mirror. "Think of things that make you happy."

She remembered her little foster sister's pleading voice, as Margo locked the back door from the outside—just before the fire raged through her foster parents' home. There Margo had been completely in control. She had planned out her whole escape and then carried out the plan without a hitch.

She laughed wickedly. *A fire was about the best thing that could have happened to that tacky place. Anyone who would paint a living-room wall orange deserves to have it incinerated to a nasty, smelly, black heap of charcoal.*

For a little brat, Nina hadn't been that awful, Margo admitted. But she was young and weak. Her death had been necessary to Margo's master plan. *And a master planner never lets human weakness get in her way.*

She smiled triumphantly. "I can do it this time, too," she said to her reflection in the cracked mirror. "I can set a goal and I can reach it—without any help from anyone."

Georgie's death, now—that carried a real feeling of accomplishment. It was amazing that a kid so young had already become such a fat, disgusting little wimp. Margo remembered the strength she'd felt coursing through her arms as she'd held his round little head under in the lake. His struggling was too weak to cause more than a tiny ripple in the surface of the water.

"It was too easy!" Margo announced gleefully. "Just once, I'd like a worthy opponent!"

Josh, said the voice in her head. The voice carried a tone of warning, but Margo thrust it aside. Georgie's older brother had been following her west, but Margo was sure she'd managed to elude him in Los Angeles. At first, she'd found Josh Smith attractive, with his intriguing, fair-haired good looks. But Josh had turned out to be a self-righteous bore. Besides, he had been off-limits, even when Margo was still in Ohio. Margo didn't believe in mixing work and pleasure.

As soon as she became Elizabeth Wakefield, she'd be able to have any guy in Sweet Valley. And it was a sure bet that the Wakefields' living room wasn't painted orange!

Margo frowned at her raven-haired reflection in the mirror. This was her natural hair color— before she'd lightened it. Now she whipped off the dark wig and tossed it onto the dresser. She yanked out a few bobby pins and watched, entranced, as her own hair swung loose around her face—as golden as California sunshine. *Just like Jessica Wakefield's.*

But Margo needed to look like Elizabeth, not Jessica. Margo knew the twins preferred different hairstyles. She deftly pulled back locks of hair above her ears, as if she were going to hold them in place with barrettes. Margo smiled. She looked exactly like Elizabeth. Of course, it was still too soon to become Elizabeth. But it was just about time to create Marla Field.

The pounding in her head had eased up a bit. She turned to the bed, where she had spread out her disguises earlier.

Margo chose a brown, curly wig and a pair of large-framed glasses, the tinted kind that turn

31

darker in sunlight. She was already collecting copies of the clothes she'd seen both of the twins wearing. But it was too soon for that. As Marla, she would wear gauze skirts and loose, cotton tops. That would be inconspicuous, and different enough from either Wakefield twin to discourage comparisons. She laid out an outfit for her job interview the next morning.

Margo reached for the letter of recommendation she'd written on her rented typewriter.

"Rave reviews for Miss Marla Field, age twenty, from her former employer!" she said aloud, sitting on the edge of the bed. She scanned the letter again, reading occasional passages out loud.

"Marla was a deeply committed day-care provider . . ." she read. "Eight-year-old Georgie will never have another baby-sitter like her . . . she touched all of our lives forever . . . Georgie loved her inventive games and picnics at the lake . . . *even taught him how to swim* . . ." Margo chuckled at that line. "I'd highly recommend Marla for any job that involves taking care of children."

I take care of them, all right!

She picked up a pen and signed "Sheila Smith" in large, loopy letters across the bottom of the page.

The letter would cinch it, she decided, laying the sheet of paper on her pillow. By this time tomorrow, she'd have a job at Little Darlings Day Care. And she was sure the little darlings would be quite helpful in relaying information on the Wakefields and the other families of Sweet Valley, California.

Margo walked across the room and stared at her reflection in the mirror. Elizabeth's blond hair and blue eyes were hers. Now those eyes glinted with a cold, intense light.

Her life will be yours, whispered the voice inside her brain.

"Her life will be mine," whispered Margo.

Chapter 3

"I just love little children!" Margo said enthusiastically the next morning, poking at her large-framed glasses to push them higher on her nose.

"So do I, dear," replied the grandmotherly woman who was the manager of Little Darlings Day Care. "It's so rewarding when they look up at you with those sweet, innocent eyes. . . ."

Margo smiled sweetly. "They're so *trusting*," she said, savoring the way that last word rolled off her tongue. Manipulating people gave Margo a heady rush of power, and she knew that Mrs. Waverly would take every word Margo said in exactly the way Margo wanted her to.

The old bag is eating out of the palm of my hand. All I've got to do is humor the fat old cow by smiling a lot and waxing poetic about the sniveling little carpet slugs. Another two minutes of this, and I'll have this job sewn up.

"I just love watching small children play—" Mrs. Waverly was saying.

With matches, Margo almost replied aloud. *Come on, lady, get to the point. I don't have all day.*

"Well, Marla, I can see that you share my love of children. That's the most important qualification for employment here at Little Darlings. And your references are quite impressive. Your last charge, Georgie Smith, sounds like such a dear. I can tell from her letter that his poor mother was just devastated when you left Ohio."

"I'll always have fond memories of Georgie," said Margo, wistfully twirling a curl of her dark brown wig, and allowing her eyes to get just a tad misty.

"You said you'd be able to start work here immediately," said Mrs. Waverly. "And it can't be too soon for me! We're quite shorthanded, you know. You could save me a lot of worry if you could start as soon as tomorrow morning. No, what am I thinking? I couldn't possibly ask you to start sooner—"

"Tomorrow would be perfect," Margo interrupted.

"Lovely!" said Mrs. Waverly. "Of course,

that's contingent upon a phone call to your last employer—we're required to do that, you know."

Margo thought fast.

"I am so sorry, Mrs. Waverly, but the Smiths are out of the country. Mrs. Smith is an antiques dealer. She's in England for a month, looking for—uh, Victorian jewelry. She'll be home in three weeks."

"I see," said Mrs. Waverly. "Well, there's no reason why we should hold up your employment here on a technicality. If you don't mind, we'll start you out tomorrow as a temporary employee. After I call Mrs. Smith in three weeks, we can switch you to permanent status. Will that be all right?"

"That will be just fine," Margo agreed. Three weeks would be plenty of time. By the time Mrs. Waverly found out that the Smith number was phony, Margo—and Marla—would be long gone from Little Darlings Day Care.

And the Wakefield family would have a new Elizabeth.

That afternoon, Elizabeth walked slowly along the sidewalk, lost in thought. School was over for the day, and she was heading home in the bright sunlight. The day looked normal—lovely, really. But something in the bright blue of the sky made her uneasy. And the sunlight felt cold. It reminded her of something she couldn't quite remember.

Elizabeth vaguely noticed a car pull to a stop nearby. Then, a familiar voice drew her out of her thoughts.

"Elizabeth!" called Jessica, leaning out the window of the Jeep. "I can give you a ride home if you want. After all, we *are* going in the same direction. . . ."

Jessica smiled tentatively, and Elizabeth felt her own tension melt away. Suddenly, the sunlight felt warm and normal again.

She grinned back at her sister, a little shyly. It had been weeks since she and Jessica had smiled at each other. Maybe Jessica was almost ready to forgive Elizabeth for Sam's death.

"Sure, Jess," Elizabeth said. "I'd love a ride home."

Elizabeth had not been in the twins' Jeep since the night of the accident. First it had been in the repair shop for some time. And with Elizabeth's driver's license revoked, and the twins' relationship strained, the Jeep had been Jessica's domain since that terrible night.

Now, Elizabeth suppressed a shudder as she climbed in on the passenger's side.

She supposed she would never know what

had really happened the night of the Jungle Prom. Oh, she knew what the police and various witnesses had said, but she still remembered very little of the dance, and nothing of what had happened afterward.

Elizabeth didn't drink. Neither did Sam. She didn't know where they had gotten the alcohol; she didn't remember seeing any liquor at the dance. And she didn't know why she had left the dance with her sister's boyfriend.

"Are you okay, Liz?" Jessica asked.

Elizabeth jumped. "I'm sorry," she said, forcing a laugh. "It's just a little strange to be back in the Jeep again."

"Yeah," Jessica said awkwardly. "But it's good to have you here again. I mean—it can be pretty boring, driving home alone, with nobody to complain to about the latest pop quiz in French class!"

"I'm glad I'm good for something," Elizabeth said, grinning. "Liz Wakefield—punching bag, sounding board, and complaint department!"

Jessica drove in silence for a few minutes, staring intently at the road in front of the Jeep.

"So, Liz," she began haltingly. "Have you decided what you're going to wear to Olivia's costume party Saturday night?"

Elizabeth shook her head, grateful for her sister's attempt at normal conversation. "I haven't the slightest idea," she admitted. "Enid and I are trying to think of some really creative costumes, but nothing comes to mind. What about you?"

"I haven't decided either," Jessica said. "Amy's going to be Cleopatra," she continued quickly.

"That ought to be good," Elizabeth answered. *This is going nowhere*, she chastised herself. She finally had a chance to talk with Jessica—to really talk—and she was blowing it. She turned to look at her sister's face in profile, so much like her own.

Elizabeth took a deep breath. "How have things been with you, Jess?" she ventured in a serious tone.

"Okay," Jessica said, turning to glance at her gratefully. Elizabeth realized that Jessica had been trying just as hard to break through the awkwardness that hung between them.

"I—I don't know," Jessica continued in a rush. "I feel better about myself, since James . . ."

Jessica's voice trailed off, and Elizabeth stared at her profile, perplexed.

"But, Jess," she said softly, "you had no reason to feel bad about yourself. I don't know what was happening between you and Sam that night, but I'm the one who—"

"Don't blame yourself, Elizabeth!" Jessica interrupted. "The accident wasn't your fault."

"Thanks, Jess," Elizabeth said quietly. "You're the one person I've really wanted to hear that from." She thought for a moment, and then continued slowly. "But I have to take some responsibility," she said, "even though the judge acquitted me. Sam's death was at least partly my fault. I'm learning to live with that. If I was drinking, then I had no business driving. I should have known—"

"You had no way of knowing, Liz," said Jessica as she stopped the Jeep at a red light. She opened her mouth again as if she had more to say, but then closed it and shook her head.

Elizabeth wondered what her sister had been about to say. She was sure she had seen a look of guilt in Jessica's green-blue eyes. But what did Jessica have to blame herself for? Elizabeth decided that Jessica must be feeling guilty about having dated Todd a few times since the night of the accident.

But I don't own Todd, Elizabeth thought, trying to convince herself that she didn't care who he dated. Her relationship with him was over. At least now she had reason to hope that things between her and Jessica might improve.

The light turned green, and Jessica moved

the car forward through the intersection.

"What about Todd?" Jessica asked gently.

"How did you know I was thinking about him?" Elizabeth asked, surprised.

"Twins know," said Jessica simply, looking over at her sister.

"Jess, I'm through with Todd forever," Elizabeth said seriously. "Todd blew it. He abandoned me when I needed him most."

Jessica looked away again.

"Jessica," Elizabeth said, "I'm not mad anymore about you and Todd. . . ."

Elizabeth bit her lip, realizing that her last words weren't quite true. Maybe she'd been deceiving herself. Maybe she still was a little angry. But she'd get over it. Her relationship with Jessica was more important.

The silence between the sisters seemed strained, and Elizabeth was relieved when Jessica changed the subject.

"Did you notice that Winston wasn't in school today?"

"Yes, I looked for him in history class," Elizabeth said. "You know, his parents left town this weekend. I hope he's okay—"

"Same old Liz!" Jessica said, laughing. Then she stopped abruptly. "And I'm glad," she added quickly, pulling the Jeep into the driveway of the

Wakefield house. "If I know Winston, he's taking advantage of his parents' being away," Jessica said, pulling her keys from the ignition. "I bet he'll play hooky all week! Can't you see him right now, hanging out on the beach, having the time of his life. . . ."

"Come on, Daisy," Winston was urging at that moment. "I'm supposed to be living it up—not tearing my hair out, trying to change a diaper. I know I've done this at least five times since yesterday, but I still can't get it right. Help me out!"

Winston was kneeling next to the coffee table in the living room, trying to shove a disposable diaper under the business end of the baby, who lay on her back on the carpet, squirming like mad and staring up at him with a quizzical expression.

He stopped in frustration. "You've got to meet me halfway, rug rat! How am I supposed to get this thing under you?"

Daisy let out a howl.

"We've been through this every time, kid. I only have two hands. You've got to stop trying to kick me in the face. How am I supposed to keep you still, hold your feet up in the air, *and* get the diaper on you?"

Daisy's response was to begin crying in earnest.

43

"Why does a baby cry?" Winston asked with a sigh, trying to stay calm. "Because it's either wet or hungry, right? Well, the dirty diaper is off, rug rat, and I'm trying to put the dry one on you. You couldn't be hungry—you just had some milk. I know it was just regular milk—but your loony mother only left enough formula for the night. Where is she? She should've been back hours ago!"

Daisy's little face was turning pink.

"Please stop crying," Winston begged. "Please, please, please stop crying!" He rapped his own forehead with his fist, trying to remember everything he'd ever heard about babies; his cousin Allie had been Daisy's age not too long ago. She and her parents had visited once or twice. What was it that Aunt Sarah did to make her stop crying.

"I know," he remembered. "The pacifier! You plug the kid's mouth, and the kid stops crying."

He held on to the baby with one hand and rooted around in the hippopotamus bag with the other. "Where is that little plastic thing?"

He picked up the bag in desperation and threw it across the room. "I can't do this!" he cried. "Why did I let your wacky mother talk me into this, Daisy? Why?"

Daisy was crying even louder now, and her face was bright red.

"I'm sorry, rug rat," Winston said. "I know you're not crying just to freak me out, but I don't know how to help you. I just don't *do* babies— you know what I mean?"

He sighed. "Let's try this diaper thing again, Daisy." Winston picked the baby up and held her in one arm while he laid the diaper on the carpet, thinking that he could then put her down on the diaper, instead of putting the diaper on her.

"That's it, Daisy," he said, as he struggled to pull the diaper around the baby's legs. "One tape down . . . *Rats!*"

Daisy had kicked Winston squarely in the face, sending his thick glasses spinning across the room. Suddenly, she stopped crying and smiled broadly.

Winston sat back on his heels and shook his head. The room was blurry, but he couldn't search for his glasses and keep the baby from scooting away.

"I can't believe this is happening to me," he said. "Pinch me, Daisy, and maybe I'll wake up!"

He pulled his hand away from her grasping fingers. "Forget I suggested that," he said quickly, squinting to see her.

"Goo-boo dee boo boo," Daisy responded in a tone that exactly matched Winston's.

"Just because you give me that big smile that

45

shows off your one little tooth doesn't mean I'll forgive you for crying like a banshee all afternoon. What do you think I am—a pushover?"

Daisy cooed.

"Okay, so I'm a pushover," Winston admitted.

Daisy grabbed Winston's finger and enclosed it in her tiny, perfect fist.

"I think you've got this the wrong way around, Daisy," he told her with a sigh. "*I'm* the one who's wrapped around *your* little finger."

The doorbell rang and Winston jumped to his feet. "What am I supposed to do now?" He stared around the room in a panic. "I know—hide the baby!"

He snatched up the infant as if she were a fumbled ball, and ran across the living room to the closet in the entrance foyer. On the way, he nearly tripped over something that had to be the hippopotamus bag.

"My glasses!" he cried, regaining his footing. "I can't see a thing without my glasses."

He turned and scrambled back across the carpet to the far side of the living room. He dropped to his knees to feel around for the glasses, still clutching the baby in one hand.

The doorbell rang again.

"Just a minute!" Winston yelled. Then he felt something under his left knee.

"I think I found my glasses," he said. He slipped them on, simultaneoulsy trying to straighten them out, and struggled to his feet. As he did, he noticed that the arm on which Daisy was perched felt warm and damp.

"Daisy, how could you?" he screamed.

Daisy fluttered her eyelashes.

Winston ran back toward the front door, opened the coat closet, and then changed his mind. He couldn't leave a baby in a closet, could he?

"I've got it!" he said. He spun around and headed for the sofa, which somehow didn't look quite as white as it had been the day before. "Under the couch!"

He shook his head. "No, Winston, you idiot. She's a baby, not a dust bunny."

He eyed a large, empty vase on the mantel, but rejected the idea. She'd never fit.

The doorbell rang again. "Winston!" came the muffled voice of his girlfriend, Maria Santelli. "I know you're in there! Is everything okay?"

"I'll be right there!" he yelled.

He ran back to the door and skidded on Daisy's plastic pacifier, which was lying on the tiled floor of the entranceway. He turned just in time to hit the wall, painfully, with the back of his shoulder. Daisy clapped her hands together and cooed appreciatively.

"I give up!" said Winston. He opened the closet door and yanked his parka off its hanger. Scrunching it into a bed on the closet floor, he gently laid Daisy on it.

"Shhh!" he cautioned in a whisper, putting one finger to his lips. "You be quiet until I get rid of her, Daisy." He turned on the closet light, closed the door, and leaned against it for a moment, grateful to hear a low, happy gurgling inside. He didn't think it was loud enough for Maria to notice, unless she stood against the door. He just hoped Daisy would stay put.

Winston jumped as the doorbell rang again. He leaped forward and grabbed the doorknob, but had the presence of mind to turn to inspect the living room for any signs of babyness.

"Rats!" he yelled. He sprinted across the floor, grabbed the hippopotamus bag, and hurled it into the dining room. Then he picked up the wet diaper and pushed it under the sofa. On his way back to the door he reached for the pacifier he had stepped on and stuck it in his pocket.

The doorbell rang again, and Maria's voice came through loud and clear. "Winston, are you all right?"

He bounded across the room, opened the door gallantly, and welcomed Maria with a flourish.

48

"Why, hello, Maria," he said, trying not to pant. "How nice to see you!"

"I was worried about you when you didn't show up at school today."

He shrugged nervously, stepping forward to keep himself between Maria and the coat closet as she walked into the foyer. "You know how it is," he said. "I thought I'd take advantage of my parents' being away, and, you know, just hang out. . . ."

"That's not like you at all, Winston," said Maria, tossing back her dark hair. She scanned the room—*sniffing like a bloodhound,* thought Winston—and then wrinkled her nose. "What's that smell?" she asked.

"What smell?" Winston asked. "Oh, *that* smell. I guess I forgot to take out the garbage." He shrugged again. "You know how it is, with the parents away. . . . Well, it was nice of you to stop by and check on me, but I'm all right, really. So I won't keep you here any longer—"

"Winston, there's something you're not telling me!" Maria said. Then she laughed. "Have you got another girl stashed away here?"

Suddenly Daisy started to wail—loudly. Maria looked puzzled. "I've heard of cradle robbing . . ." she began.

Winston sighed. "Okay, you might as well

know the truth," he said, opening the closet door. "I guess I could use some help, anyway. Just promise me you won't tell anybody. Me— changing diapers! If anyone found out, I'd be the laughingstock of Sweet Valley High!"

But Maria wasn't listening. She was on her knees, cuddling the pink-and-gold baby and babbling softly in what sounded to Winston like gibberish.

"I can't believe it," Winston grumbled under his breath, shaking his head at Maria, who paid him no attention. "Just one look at a baby, and you lose every shred of dignity."

Josh Smith squinted into the late-afternoon sunlight. In the distance, lush green hills rose under a spotless Sweet Valley blue sky.

Josh had arrived that morning and had checked into a motel. Now he was taking a walk to familiarize himself with the town.

He gazed around at the quiet, tree-lined street. The shops and restaurants were brightly painted; their doors stood open, invitingly. Young people, their clothing as colorful as the feathers of parrots, laughed and talked as they strolled along the sidewalks—probably on their way home from a nearby high school, Josh figured.

He stared carefully at every girl who passed

by. The age was about right, he decided. But he didn't see her—not here, not yet. He hadn't really expected to, so soon. But he knew Margo was nearby. He could feel it.

It was a beautiful place. Everybody looked happy and relaxed, but Josh frowned. He couldn't bear the thought of this lovely town becoming another site of Margo's murder and vengeance.

He balled both of his hands into fists and made a silent vow. This time, he would stop Margo—if it was the last thing he did.

Chapter 4

"I know who you look like, Marla!" boasted four-year-old Angie Amadi on the playground at Little Darlings Day Care. She held her hands linked behind her back as she looked up at the new teacher's aide.

"Who?" asked Margo, not believing her luck.

"It's a secret."

"If you tell me your secret, I'll tell you mine."

"OK," Angie agreed happily. "You look like the two girls that live on my street. I live on Calico Drive—Mommy made me remember it in case I get lost. The two girls are teenagers! They look just like each other, and just like you, too. Except that they have straight yellow hair and you have curly brown hair."

"Do you know their names?" Margo asked.

"Yep," said Angie proudly. "Jessica and Elizabeth. They come over to baby-sit me sometimes. They're pretty, and they have a big dog named Prince Albert. I have a cat named Kitty. Do you have a cat?"

"No, I don't have a cat," said Margo. "Prince Albert, huh? Is Prince Albert a mean dog?"

Angie giggled. "Nope. I pet him sometimes when they take him for a walk. Their daddy says he's really a pussycat. Isn't that funny? Prince Albert is a dog but their daddy says he's a cat. He's funny."

"He must be very nice if he stops to talk to little girls," Margo said.

"Yep. My mommy says him and Mrs. Wakefield are about the nicest people in town!"

"What else does your mommy say about Mr. and Mrs. Wakefield?"

"She said they were gonna get a divorce once. My mommy got a divorce. Mr. Wakefield moved away, but he came back. And now they aren't gonna get a divorce."

"How terrible," said Margo, feigning shock. "I'm glad they aren't going to get a divorce anymore."

"I told you my secret," Angie interrupted. "Now you tell me your secret, Marla."

"This whole little talk is my secret," said Margo. The girl turned her head. "What?"

"Well, you told me about the Wakefield family. Let's make that a secret. Nobody else will know that we had this little talk. It'll be *our* secret. Can you keep a secret?"

"I think so," said Angie, grinning.

"You think so?" Margo asked sharply. "Do you know what happens to little girls who can't keep secrets?"

Angie shook her head slowly, eyes wide. Margo crossed her arms and glared at the little girl, enjoying the effect. Angie put a lock of her black, curly hair into her mouth and sucked on it, hard, as she stared up at Margo.

"Sometimes, their kittens get drowned," Margo said darkly. "But if they tell a *really important* secret, little girls can get all burned up!"

A tear ran down Angie's face. "I can keep a secret, Marla. I'm sure I can."

"You know, Angie. This is a really important secret!"

"I won't tell anyone," Angie said solemnly. "I promise!"

Suddenly, Margo was all smiles. "I knew you wouldn't tell," she said. "You and me are going to be great friends!"

Angie smiled back with a mixture of adoration and terror.

"Aren't kids wonderful?" Margo said aloud to

no one in particular. "I think I'm going to like working here!"

Elizabeth sat at her desk that evening, catching up on some homework.

"Elizabeth?" Jessica asked tentatively, stepping into Elizabeth's room through the door from the twins' bathroom. "Would you mind if I borrowed your new cotton sweater? The one that matches my—uh, *our* eyes? I hate to ask, but I'm going out with James, and the sweater I wanted to wear has ketchup stains on it from the Dairi Burger the other night."

Elizabeth shook her head, laughing. "I never thought I'd hear myself saying it," she said, "but it's *great* having you poke your head in here, without knocking, to ask if you can wear everything in my closet. It's just like old times!"

Jessica sighed, relieved. "Yes, it is great," she agreed. "And it expands my wardrobe potential immensely. Does that mean I can borrow the sweater?"

"Well—" Elizabeth began slowly, trying to cover a grin. "Do you promise not to get it dirty? And to wash it and fold it *neatly*—by tomorrow?"

"You weren't kidding when you said this was just like old times!"

Elizabeth walked to her closet, pulled the

new sweater off a neatly arranged shelf, and held it up. "But there's one more condition," she said.

Jessica sighed impatiently. "What now?"

Elizabeth tossed her the sweater. "No ketchup!" she said.

Jessica giggled as the sweater hit her in the face. "It's a deal! I won't eat anything that isn't the exact same shade of blue-green as this sweater," she promised after she had undraped it from around her neck. "You know," she said, changing the subject suddenly. "Lila is having a bunch of friends over on Saturday afternoon for ice cream. It'll be kind of a pre-costume-party bash—"

"I know," Elizabeth said. "She invited me— through Enid, of all people."

"She did?" Jessica asked. "Through Enid?"

"Yeah, I know. Since when are Lila and Enid even *talking* to each other?"

Jessica beamed, and Elizabeth smiled back. She suspected that her own friends and Jessica's friends, as different as they were, had come together in an attempt to bring the twins together again. Obviously, the cold war had been hard on everyone.

"You're going, aren't you?" Jessica prodded.

Elizabeth shrugged. "To tell you the truth, I wasn't planning to. I didn't think you'd be too thrilled to have me there."

"But I'd really like it if you came, Liz," she said, brushing at an imaginary speck on the sweater.

She looked up, and Elizabeth smiled at her. "OK, then. I'll plan on it."

The doorbell rang and Jessica jumped. "Oh, no!" she cried. "It's James, and I'm not ready!"

Elizabeth watched, laughing, as her sister ran out of the room. "Same old Jess!" she called after her. Maybe things really were going back to normal.

Five minutes later, Elizabeth heard Jessica greeting James. When the door shut behind them, Elizabeth walked to her window to see Jessica—stunning in the blue sweater and a pair of tight black jeans—strolling down the front walkway with James's arm around her waist. Jessica smiled radiantly as he gazed down at her, and they laughed together at something he said.

Elizabeth turned away. "I'm happy for her—really I am," she said aloud. "But I'd like to go out with someone special, too."

Her mind drifted to the Fowler wedding. She had gazed into Todd's deep brown eyes and felt his strong arms around her. . . .

"No!" she told herself. "Not Todd. He blew it! He proved that he doesn't care anymore."

"It's almost like having a whole new wardrobe,"

Jessica explained to James as they sat in a back booth at the Dairi Burger. "It's been ages since Elizabeth has let me borrow a sweater! For a few minutes in her room tonight, it was just like old times."

She paused so that James would ask her to continue, as he always did, but he picked up his milk shake instead and took a long sip. Jessica shrugged and continued speaking.

"I had thought we'd never be close again. I was so angry, and I felt so bad about what I did—"

She stopped, flustered. "I just felt so bad," she concluded. She looked down at the french fry she was absentmindedly dragging through the dollop of ketchup on her plate—Elizabeth would never know, she had figured, as long as she was careful with the sweater.

Jessica liked the way James always hung on her every word, always wanting to know more. But now she wasn't sure how she would answer him if he asked her why she felt bad. She'd tried for so long not to think about what she'd done . . . about how she had secretly spiked Elizabeth's drink the night of the dance.

But James didn't ask. Jessica felt confused, but she pushed the nagging fear to the back of her mind and continued with a smile.

"I know it may be hard for other people to understand, but my relationship with Elizabeth is the most important thing in my life. It sounds corny, but being twins is like being two halves of the same person. Sometimes we even pick up on each other's feelings."

James narrowed his eyes. "You mean like telepathy?" he asked skeptically.

"Not exactly. It's just a feeling I get sometimes that Elizabeth is in trouble. Like the time she was kidnapped. I was at a party, Elizabeth was late, and I had this nagging feeling that something was wrong."

"That's amazing," said James. "What did you do?"

Jessica looked at the table and shook her head. "Not enough," she admitted. "There was this guy I wanted to impress, so I kept ignoring the feelings I was having about Elizabeth—until Todd shoved me into the pool! He made me realize that something was really wrong. But we eventually managed to rescue her."

James took her hand. "I hope she wasn't too mad that you ignored what you were sensing."

"Not Elizabeth," Jessica said firmly. "She was just grateful that I helped find her. Usually, Elizabeth is the one who gets *me* out of trouble. I don't know what I'd do without Elizabeth. She's my anchor."

James listened thoughtfully but didn't reply.

Jessica was stumped. It wasn't that James was ignoring her. Not at all. He'd been completely attentive the entire evening—kinder and sweeter than usual, even. He let her choose the movie, and he'd even squeezed her hand when she cried during the sad part—instead of making a joke out of it, as Sam used to do.

After the movie, James had walked around the mall with her, waiting patiently while she admired a dress at Bibi's and fell in love with a shimmering scarf at the Lytton & Brown department store. Sam had always hated going shopping with her—even window shopping.

But James had been quieter than he usually was on their dates, and he didn't seem as curious to know everything about her. *Is he losing interest?* Jessica felt her heart racing desperately at the thought. She couldn't bear to lose James now.

No, she told herself, trying not to think about the hike in the mountains and the steep ravine beneath her feet. *There's nothing to worry about. James loves me.*

"Are you okay?" Jessica asked him, leaning across the table toward him. "You seem a little— I don't know, quiet or something. Am I boring you?"

He smiled gently and traced the lines of her face with his finger. "Never," he said. "I'm just a little tired. Let's call it an early night, OK? I've got an early practice tomorrow. . . ."

Jessica smiled back. "Sure," she agreed. But she had the distinct impression that James was lying.

Elizabeth paced around her bedroom.

She glanced over at her desk. There was the soccer article she'd been editing for *The Oracle*, Sweet Valley High's student newspaper. Sports wasn't Elizabeth's usual beat, but she was helping her friend Penny Ayala, the editor-in-chief. It felt good to be "dependable Liz, the writer," again. In fact, she was getting a lot of satisfaction these days out of the little details of her life that she had taken for granted before the accident and its aftermath.

"Almost having to spend six months in reform school will do that to you," she said wryly, still pacing.

But Elizabeth was too restless to sit still and edit a story about the upcoming soccer playoffs. And she had finished all her homework before dinner. She looked around the room, searching for something else to keep her occupied. As usual, everything was in perfect order.

"Laundry!" she said suddenly. She had been meaning to do a load for two days now. She stopped in front of the mirror and addressed herself. "Jessica is out on a date, and I'm home doing laundry." She shook her head. "Liz, you're a wild woman!"

As long as she was doing a load of laundry, Elizabeth decided she might as well throw in some of Jessica's stuff, too.

She remembered the beach party months earlier—before the Jungle Prom and its tragic aftermath—where she had promised to stop looking after Jessica and start putting herself first. "Well," she told her reflection. "Old habits die hard!" But she was smiling as she said it.

Elizabeth stood in the middle of Jessica's room a few minutes later, shaking her head. It had been a long time since she'd been in her sister's room. It almost felt good to be standing ankle deep in the layer of debris that always covered Jessica's bedroom carpet.

"I never thought I'd be feeling nostalgic for all this," she told herself with a smile, gesturing around the room. "How does she find anything in here?" She knelt down and slipped her hand under a stack of *Ingenue* magazines—to yank out the infamous ketchup-stained sweater that was underneath them.

"That's easy," she said, answering her own question. "She doesn't find anything in here. She comes to me and borrows whatever she can't put her hands on in her own room."

She reached for a pair of psychedelic stirrup pants that were entwined around the bottom of a bedpost. As she tugged them loose, a wrinkled envelope sprang out from under the bed.

"That's just like Jessica," she said. "Losing a letter in this mess . . ."

Elizabeth lifted the envelope off the floor and was about to toss it on top of the jumble of papers on Jessica's desk, when the name on the envelope caught her eye.

It was her own name, and the handwriting was Todd's.

Elizabeth dropped the stirrup pants and pulled out the letter. It was dated two weeks earlier.

"'I'm watching the sunset, Elizabeth,'" she read aloud, "'and I wish I could write as well as you do, so I could tell you how beautiful it is, because beautiful sights always make me think of you—'"

She collapsed onto the bed, not caring that she was crushing the half-dozen blouses that Jessica must have tried on before deciding what to wear that night.

Elizabeth read quickly, tears forming in her eyes.

"I can't believe it," she marveled, when she had finished the letter. "Todd still loves me. He always loved me! And he wants to know if *I* forgive *him*!"

Elizabeth stared at the page in disbelief for a minute. Then she reread the last paragraph, aloud:

"'I can't believe I've wasted so much time, Liz—time we could have spent together. I wanted to be there for you. I've been too blinded by pride and jealousy and anger. It may be too late, but I had to let you know that you are the only person I have ever loved. I don't blame you if you never want to see me again. . . .'"

Elizabeth looked up, trying to control the storm of emotions that whirled inside her. Todd still loved her, and she knew in her heart that she had never stopped loving him.

But Jessica had betrayed her. Jessica had known about the letter but had kept it from her. Elizabeth pounded the pillow with her fist. How could Jessica do that to her? Why would she want to hurt her like that?

Elizabeth threw herself against the pillow, sobbing.

So much love. So much wasted time.

James pushed open the door of Kelly's Bar and scanned the smoky room. He'd dropped Jessica off at home and headed straight there.

"Hey, dude!" called a familiar voice. Leroy, one of the bar regulars, sat on his usual stool at the corner of the bar. "Where you been lately, Jimmy boy?" he said, slurring his words. "You gone uptown on us?"

James waved without looking toward him. Then he spotted Margo in a booth in the back of the room. He made his way toward her—side-stepping a drunk who was dancing by himself, oblivious to the lack of music.

What a sleazy place, James thought as he slid into the booth. He shifted his weight to avoid sitting on a slit in the dirty brown vinyl. James had hung out at Kelly's for at least a year, but after an hour at the clean, light-filled Dairi Burger, this place felt like an alien planet.

Maybe I am going uptown, James mused to himself, wondering if that was good or bad.

Margo was slowly entwining a lock of her long hair around her finger. James was startled. Her hair was as black as the night sky, but the gesture was pure Jessica.

"What took you so long, James?" she asked, with a very Jessica-like pout. "I got out of *cheer-*

leader practice positively *ages* ago!"

James stared. This girl could be Jessica's twin. Heck, she could be Jessica herself. She even *sounded* like Jessica. And she was wearing a tight, bright-pink tank top that looked just like one Jessica had worn a few days earlier. *What is this sick girl up to?*

"Cut the crap, Mandy," he ordered, stifling the urge to add *or whatever your real name is.* "Besides," he added, "I'm a half hour early. It's only nine-thirty."

"I know," said Margo in her usual, expressionless voice. She stared at him with eyes that were just like Jessica's, but colder. "Why?" she demanded.

"We went to an early movie," James said. "Besides, she was getting on my nerves."

"I pay you to put up with her," Margo reminded him sharply. "I pay you to listen to her."

James put up his hand. "I know, I know," he said. "But she wasn't talking much tonight. She seemed kind of tired. So I got bored, made up an excuse, and took her home."

The bartender appeared at their table, and James was taken aback. Kelly's wasn't known for its table service. "Are you gonna order a drink?" he asked gruffly, eyes locked on Margo's tank top.

"Beer," said James. "Whatever's on draft."

Margo ran a finger slowly around the rim of her glass. Then she locked eyes with the bartender. "I'm parched," she said in a breathy voice, obviously enjoying the effect she was having on the older man. "I'll have another Wild Turkey."

"Coming right up," he said, still staring. He paused for a minute and then hurried back to the bar.

Margo laughed as he left, and James shook his head.

"You don't approve of flirting?" she asked him, leaning across the table suggestively.

"That depends," he said.

"Don't you dare judge me," she said quietly, eyes blazing with an icy fire. "You're the one pretending to like somebody while using her for your own ends."

"That's different," he said. "That's business."

"See that you keep it that way," Margo ordered. James heard an unmistakable tone of menace in her voice.

A minute later, the bartender set the drinks in front of them. He paused, gazing at Margo, but she didn't even look up.

Margo waited until he was gone before continuing. "So Jessica didn't tell you anything new tonight?" she asked. "Did she say anything about how she and Elizabeth are getting along?"

James shook his head. "No," he lied. "Just more of the same old stuff. She liked this shiny kind of shawl she saw on sale at Lytton and Brown's at the mall, but she couldn't afford it."

"A shiny shawl?" Margo asked sharply. "Where in the store?"

"I don't know," James began. Margo scowled at him, and he searched his memory. "Near the top of the escalator, I think. Close to the purses and wallets."

"Good," Margo said, narrowing her eyes. "I'll buy one, and you can give it to her as a gift. That's just the kind of a guy you are. I'll get myself one exactly like it, too. It will fit in perfectly with my plan."

"I don't get it."

"Never mind," Margo commanded. "What else did she say?"

"Well, she talked about the cheerleaders for a while, but that was about it."

Margo mused for a moment, and James was afraid she'd seen through his lies. He didn't even know why he hesitated to tell her the truth. But he was sick and tired of the way this weird girl was manipulating him and everybody else. He wasn't afraid of her; he wasn't afraid of anything. But there was something bizarre about the way she was talking.

James didn't like to admit it, but he was beginning to feel uneasy about lying to Jessica. It wasn't that he owed anything to Jessica. But she was a nice enough kid. He even felt kind of sorry for her—losing her boyfriend like that, and now having this creepy girl spying on her.

Why was Mandy so interested in the relationship between the Wakefield twins? It wasn't his place to ask, James reminded himself. He was just a hired hand, doing an easy job and getting paid well for it. Just the same, he decided to be more careful from now on about relaying every scrap of information he learned—at least until he had some idea what she was up to.

"—the stupid little brats just can't keep their big mouths shut!" Margo was saying. She'd been telling him about the kids at the day-care center where she was working. "In two days, I've learned all sorts of interesting things," she boasted. "For instance, one kid told me that Ned Wakefield ran for mayor a few months ago. Why didn't *you* get that for me, from Jessica?"

She glared at James, but he ignored her and sipped his beer. "Why would a kid tell you something like that in the first place?"

Margo smiled, her eyes unfocused as if she were looking inside herself. James had a mental image of a black widow spider approaching

70

a fly that was ensnared in its web.

Picking up her drink, Margo drained the last of it. Then she locked eyes with James, holding his gaze for a full minute. She drew his eyes down to the empty glass clenched tightly in her hand.

"Kids are fragile little things," Margo said darkly. "They can break, if you apply pressure in the right places. I have ways of making sure they crack."

She reached across the table with her free arm and took James's hand. Her skin was cold and clammy. A shiver of disgust skated up his spine. Margo stared into his eyes as she spoke slowly, in a deep, unnatural voice.

"I can be *very* persuasive."

James wrenched his gaze away from her eyes, which were so much like Jessica's and yet so different. Her fingers clenched the cheap glass so tightly that her whitened knuckles looked like frosted shards of ice.

He heard a sharp crack.

Margo slowly unfurled her fingers. Broken glass glittered like ice cubes in her hand. From a long slash across her palm, crimson blood cascaded down her fingers and dripped soundlessly onto the tabletop.

James tore his gaze away from the blood and

raised it to Margo's face. She grinned triumphantly, her eyes glittering with an icy sheen.

Margo leaned forward, as if to kiss James on the forehead. But she stopped short and whispered to him instead.

"I can also be *very* dangerous."

Chapter 5

Elizabeth was already dressed for school when she stormed into Jessica's bedroom at seven o'clock the next morning.

"So this is what your little 'I'm feeling better' speeches have been about," Elizabeth began coldly.

"What are you talking about?" Jessica asked, sitting up in bed and rubbing her eyes.

"This!" Elizabeth yelled, shaking the letter in front of Jessica's face. "You thought you'd be sweet to me to get rid of your guilt about hiding this letter. Is that it? *Is that it?*"

Jessica opened her mouth to reply, but Elizabeth didn't give her the chance.

"I couldn't figure out what you had to feel guilty about," Elizabeth continued. "After all, *I* was the one in the Jeep when Sam died. *I* was the one who got him killed, even if I didn't kill him myself. People are making sure that *I* don't forget that."

Jessica cringed.

"But don't worry, Jess," Elizabeth said more quietly, her voice cracking with emotion. "I'll remember it as long as I live. But this—" She shook the letter in Jessica's face again. "Why would you keep it from me all this time? Why do you want to hurt me even more?"

"I don't," Jessica whispered, shaking her tousled head as tears spilled from the corners of her eyes. "It wasn't like that, Liz, I swear—"

"Oh, shut up," Elizabeth said in a hard, weary voice. "I'm sick of your lying. And I'm sick of you. I had hoped with all my heart that we could be friends—and sisters—again. But now I see that we can't."

Jessica shook her head wordlessly as Elizabeth spun on her heel and walked out of the room.

"Yes, Winston, we're having a wonderful time with your aunt Sarah and uncle Tom," crackled Sharon Egbert's voice through the telephone receiver that afternoon. "I wish you could see the baby. You wouldn't believe how big little Allie has gotten!"

Winston was sitting on his parents' bed, gripping the receiver in one hand. Daisy was making gurgling noises as she lay on her stomach on the expensive print comforter. Winston silently thanked the phone company for the lousy connection. "Shhhh!" he hissed at Daisy.

"Dah!" Daisy announced.

"What in the world is that noise I keep hearing?" Winston's mother asked.

"Just the television, Mom," he said quickly. "It's one of those game shows where people keep squealing all the time. You know, 'Wheel of Greed,' or 'The Price Is Self-Respect,' or something like that."

Daisy said something that sounded for all the world like "*greed?*" Winston looked at her for a moment, dismissed the notion, and tried to listen to what his mother was saying.

"Frankly, I was surprised to find you home from school so soon," she said. "Your father and I will be out this evening, and I wanted to touch base. I was afraid I'd only be able to leave you an answering-machine message."

"It's three thirty. I swear," Winston quipped, "you're gone for only three days, and already you've forgotten that school gets out at three. By the end of the week, I'll be lucky if you can even remember my name."

"Of course I know when school gets out," she said: "I just assumed you'd be living it up this week, with your parents out of town."

"I guess I've become hopelessly boring in my old age," Winston said. "*Daisy!*" he yelped as the baby spit up on his parents' new comforter.

"What did you say, Winston?" his mother asked.

"Um, uh, sorry, Mom. Someone on this game show just lost a thousand dollars because she couldn't come up with the name of a wildflower that begins with a *D.*"

Daisy looked up at him in admiration.

The urchin knows a brilliant cover-up when she hears it, he told himself.

Then Daisy rolled onto her stomach, laughed with delight, and spit up again.

Winston grabbed for her, lost his balance, and banged his head against the bedpost.

"Winston?" asked his mother. "Are you sure everything's all right there?"

Winston rubbed his forehead. "Couldn't be better," he said weakly.

"Well, your father's calling me to get ready," she said. "He sends his love. And don't tell him I told you, but I think you can count on a nice present when we get home."

So can you, Winston thought wryly, looking at

the milky spots of baby drool on the bedspread.

The doorbell rang, and Winston sighed gratefully. It had to be either Maria, with more diapers, or Mrs. Zvonchenko, to collect Daisy. Either way, Winston would get some relief. He ran downstairs, holding the baby carefully against his chest.

"Boy, am I glad to see you," he began, opening the door to find his girlfriend holding a package of disposable diapers.

"Oooh, she's adorable!" said Amy Sutton, pushing her way around Maria to scoop the baby out of Winston's grasp. "Let me hold her!"

So much for keeping Daisy a secret, Winston thought. Telling Amy anything was as good as announcing it on national television.

Maria handed the diapers to Winston and stepped inside after Amy. Behind her, Annie Whitman, Lila Fowler, Pamela Robertson, and Cheryl Thomas pushed their way in and crowded around Amy and the baby.

"Look at her one little tooth!" Annie squealed. "It looks like an itty-bitty little pearl. Isn't she the sweetest—"

"Uh, girls," Winston began. "Actually, I was hoping to keep this a secret—"

"Hi, Daisy," began Pamela, speaking in a high-pitched, baby-talk voice. "Kootchy-kootchykoo!" she said, tickling her gently on the tummy.

"Just promise me you won't—" Winston began again.

"I can see why they call her Daisy," Lila interrupted. "That's just what she looks like, with her cute little smile and all that strawberry-blond hair. But isn't that playsuit she's wearing kind of outdated?"

"I know, Lila," Maria agreed. "It was my little sister's, so it's nearly six years old. But Daisy only came with three outfits, and we couldn't just keep washing them over and over again."

"This calls for a trip to the mall," Lila said.

"Doesn't everything?" Winston asked dryly. Lila's shopping habits were legendary.

The girls ignored him. Winston shrugged, walked into the living room, and plopped himself down on the couch.

The doorbell rang again. When Maria opened it, Winston heard Robin Wilson, Rosa Jameson, and Sandra Bacon start cooing over Daisy.

The girls moved into the room in a big clump, as though they were all part of one big statue. *Still Life With Spit-Up Machine*, Winston mused.

"Anybody home?" called another voice from the entranceway. Winston jumped up and raced toward the door, but it wasn't Mrs. Zvonchenko.

Only another cheerleader, he thought, as Jeanie West walked in.

"You know," he announced. "I've fantasized about being here in my own house with every girl at school, but somehow, this isn't what I imagined. . . ."

"There *are* a lot of us here," Amy admitted with a giggle. "We could almost hold cheer-leading practice, right here in Winston's living room."

"Except for Jessica," said Annie, reaching out to stroke the baby's foot.

"I can't believe how soft her skin is," said Cheryl.

"Jessica's?" asked Winston.

"No, dweeb," said Cheryl, "the baby's!" She gently touched one of Daisy's rosy cheeks, and then turned to her stepsister, Annie. "How much moisturizing cream do you think it would take to do that to *my* face?"

"About a million free samples from Lytton and Brown's," Annie told her. "So what is it with Jessica? She seemed so much more upbeat lately, but all day today she acted like her best friend died—" She clapped her hand over her mouth. "Well, you know what I mean. I'm worried about her. Did she say anything to you, Lila?"

Lila shook her head. "No," she said. "In fact,

79

she hardly said a word to *anyone* at school, all day long. Not exactly normal behavior for Jessica."

"Ba bee doodle," Daisy insisted, instantly regaining her position as the center of attention.

"I've got an idea, Winston!" Maria called to him, gently rocking the baby in her arms. "Instead of going to Olivia's costume party dressed as Klingons, let's go as a threesome, with Daisy. Who could we be?"

"Lizzie Borden's parents?" Lila offered, trying to scoop the baby out of Maria's arms. Maria elbowed her away and cuddled Daisy protectively.

For some reason, Winston's knees were feeling wobbly. He walked back to the couch and lowered himself into it. A feeling of dread came over him as he sat watching Maria and the bevy of cooing girls clustered around the baby.

"You could be Popeye, Olive Oyl, and Sweet Pea," Annie suggested.

"How about Mother Nature, Father Time, and Baby New Year?" Jean asked.

"Or Tarzan, Jane, and Cheetah, the chimpanzee," Amy said dryly.

Maria scowled at her and then turned to smile at Winston.

"Isn't Daisy just the cutest thing you've ever seen in your life?"

Winston smiled back at her, but he was beginning to feel woozy.

"Isn't Winston the best?" Maria said proudly. "He's been taking care of Daisy almost all by himself for three days. He's wonderful with kids, aren't you, Winston?"

She smiled at him coyly, and Winston imagined himself ten years from now, dangling one baby on his knee as Maria stood nearby, smiling over the curly blond head of an even littler one in her arms. In his mind, a third baby sat in a nearby high chair, ceremoniously dumping strained carrots onto a shiny linoleum floor.

Babies, babies, and more babies.

Winston gripped the armrest of the sofa and stood up quickly.

"Uh, excuse me for a minute, ladies," he said. "I've got to make a phone call."

A minute later, he stood in the kitchen, holding the phone and nervously shifting his weight from one foot to the other.

"Todd, buddy, boy am I glad you're back from that basketball thing," he said into the receiver. "You've got to get over here and rescue me!"

"What's going on, Win?"

"I've got *ten women* here, and they're driving me crazy!"

Todd whistled. "And you need *rescuing?*"

"Don't ask questions. Just get over here."

"Always glad to lend a hand to a friend in need," Todd said. Winston could hear the grin in his voice. "I'm on my way!"

Winston turned, sighing loudly, and found Lila standing there, gingerly holding Daisy out in front of her. The other girls were gathered behind her, smiling expectantly.

"Uh, Winston," Lila said, wrinkling her nose. "I think little Daisy needs her diaper changed."

"She wouldn't even let me explain," Jessica was saying into a pay phone outside Sweet Valley High.

"I'm sorry, Jessica," said James. "It's too bad—just when you two were finally getting things worked out. But I can see why you held on to the letter. You were going out with the guy, after all."

"No," Jessica said, sniffing. "It was wrong of me to keep the letter from Elizabeth. She was so upset, thinking that nobody but Enid the Drip cared about her, and I let her go on believing that Todd hated her, too. How could I do that to my own sister, after everything else I've put her through?"

"Ah, Jess," James said in a soothing voice. "You've got to stop blaming yourself for everything that's happened."

"But it's my fault, James. *Everything* is my fault!" Jessica said, crying. "I don't deserve to have Elizabeth as a sister. I didn't deserve Sam, and I don't deserve you!"

"Calm down, honey," said James. "Elizabeth was driving the car the night Sam died—not you. And you went out with Todd only after you thought he and Elizabeth were through. You couldn't have known they were still in love."

"Yes, I could have," Jessica said. "I knew it all along and just didn't want to admit it. I wanted to make Elizabeth pay for what happened to Sam. I should have given her the letter."

"Why didn't you?" James asked gently.

Jessica shook her head hopelessly. "I don't know. Elizabeth and I were finally getting along, and I guess I didn't want to ruin it. And then I forgot about it altogether. How could I be so rotten?"

"You made a mistake—that's all. You have to talk to Elizabeth. You have to make her listen."

Jessica shook her head again. "I can't," she whispered.

"Yes, you can," James said gently. "But first you have to forgive yourself."

"I can't," Jessica whispered again. She held her palm over the telephone receiver and fought to control her tears. Then she took a deep breath. "I have to go, James," she said quickly. "I promised my mother I'd pick up some groceries on my way home."

"Are you sure you're OK?"

Jessica nodded. "Yes," she said in a voice that sounded more definite than she felt.

"Trust me," James said. "It will all work out."

Jessica hung up the phone slowly. "I do," she whispered. "But it won't."

It was over, Jessica knew. She had blown any chance for a reconciliation with Elizabeth. The twins were lost to each other, forever.

"What newspaper did you say you were from?" the police sergeant asked again, standing by a file cabinet in the quiet squad room of the Sweet Valley police station.

Josh drummed his fingers on the scratched surface of the table where he was seated. "The Sacramento—"

"Ah, the *Bee*," said Sergeant O'Riley, nodding. He leaned over to riffle through a file drawer. "A fine newspaper, but I've always wondered why it's got such a silly name."

He straightened up to look at Josh, who blushed under his open gaze.

"Um, I don't know, really," Josh stammered, thinking quickly. "Actually, I'm new there. In fact, this is my first big story."

What is wrong with me? Josh asked himself. *Why am I so shaky? I'm not the one who's done something illegal.*

At least, he didn't *think* it was illegal to pretend to be a newspaper reporter. He didn't know how else to get the information he needed.

"Your first story?" Sergeant O'Riley asked kindly. "I thought as much. You seem pretty nervous for a newspaperman."

"Sorry," Josh said sheepishly, relieved. "I've never even been inside a police station." He pulled out a notebook and tried to look official. "So what can you tell me about violent crimes in Sweet Valley?"

"As I said, it's a good, safe place to live," the officer assured him. "Not much here for an article on violent crime in small towns."

The sergeant poked at a file. "Of course, there was that tragic accident, not long ago, where the boy from Bridgewater was killed. But it was a drunk-driving accident, and the guy who caused it finally came forward. That wouldn't have anything to do with what you're looking for."

The sergeant pulled out another file, and Josh saw his eyes cloud over. "There was a terrible hit-and-run killing of a young woman, over in

Ramsbury just a couple of weeks ago," he said, grimacing.

Josh sat up at attention.

"Sorry, but I really can't tell you anything more about that one," the detective said apologetically. He pointed to the file. "All it says here is that it's unsolved. And it gives the name of the investigating officer. It took place outside of my precinct. You'll have to talk to a detective in the next county."

Josh could barely contain his agitation. When he scrawled something on the first page of his notebook, the pressure of his hand caused the pen to slash right through the paper. As he stood to thank the sergeant, Josh flipped the notebook cover over the page, concealing the large, black letters that spelled out one word: *Margo*.

Chapter 6

Margo hopped off the bus at the end of Calico Drive. As she watched it pull away, she tucked her light-pink T-shirt into her faded Levi's and gazed around her with satisfaction.

"My new neighborhood," she said happily, spreading her arms wide as she began walking the three blocks to the Wakefield house.

She leaned over to check out her face in the side-view mirror of a green Volvo that was parked along the street. The contact lenses made her eyes sparkle with the blue-green of the Pacific Ocean. Her long, golden hair, pulled back in barrettes, looked completely natural. Nobody would ever guess that it had been lightened.

In other words, Margo looked exactly like Elizabeth Wakefield. *Margo is Elizabeth Wakefield.*

Risky, said a voice inside her head. *Risky.*

"No!" Margo said aloud. Nobody would know. Nobody could know. What could be more natural than Elizabeth Wakefield, deprived of driving privileges—*temporarily, Margo was sure*—jumping off the bus, walking into her very own, beautiful, split-level home on Calico Drive, and seeing Alice, her very own, beautiful, wonderful, perfect mother?

Not yet, the voice told her.

"I don't care," she whispered resolutely, pounding her right fist, rhythmically, into her left palm. "She's my mother and it's my home. Or they will be mine, soon enough. I have to see my mother. I have to hear her voice. I *have* to."

Patience.

She would be careful. The outfit she was wearing was exactly right. Margo had seen Elizabeth wearing a T-shirt the same color. Her imitation of Elizabeth's voice wasn't quite perfect yet. But as long as she didn't talk too much, she'd be fine. Alice would never know the difference.

Something moved in the window of a Spanish-style ranch house, two blocks from the Wakefields'. Margo froze. Four-year-old Angie Amadi was waving frenetically, desperate to be noticed. Margo set her mouth in a hard line. The little girl had recognized her as Marla, the teacher's aide. She would have to be killed.

Then Margo laughed and returned the dark-haired girl's wave. *Of course.* The brat was waving at her neighbor, Elizabeth—not at her new teacher.

Risky, the low, raspy voice repeated in Margo's head.

Her headache was back, but Margo ignored it. "It's not risky," she whispered. "If anyone recognizes me, I have ways of keeping them quiet. *Permanently.*"

Margo looked back at little Angie and thought of an abandoned well she'd noticed, a mile from the day-care center. The well was close to a highway. The traffic would drown out the sound of the little girl's weak cries.

Oh, Angie was safe for now—she'd provided all sorts of helpful information, and Margo knew how to make sure she would continue to be useful. And of course, Angie had no inkling of the real identity of the "Elizabeth" she'd just waved to. But it was always good to have a plan—to be prepared for whatever might be necessary.

Margo grinned. Her headache was gone and the voice in her head was silent.

A few minutes later, Margo swung open the front door of the Wakefield home and let herself in. She heard the sound of a female voice, humming, and knew instantly that it was Alice Wakefield—her new mother.

Margo's heart leapt. For a moment, she felt dizzy. She wasn't sure if she wanted to rush in and throw herself into her mother's arms, or tip-toe forward, one halting step at a time, delaying the moment she'd anticipated for so long. What if something went wrong? What if—

No. Everything would be fine. She let out a sigh of pleasure as she noticed the tastefully decorated, sunlit living room. *No orange walls here, like that last foster family had.* Margo shuddered. Then she took a deep breath and walked quickly toward the sound of Alice Wakefield's humming.

She entered the kitchen and gazed around the large, airy room. Hand-painted tiles— Spanish, Margo decided—adorned the counters. A lovely china bowl with a blue border held two bananas and an apple on the table. A gleaming set of knives beckoned from the counter to Margo's left. *What I couldn't do with those,* she thought idly.

Then Margo stopped, heart pounding, at her first sight of her mother.

Alice's back was toward Margo. She was lean-ing into the open refrigerator, rummaging through a drawer full of vegetables. She wore a simple but elegant silk blouse and a straight, deep purple skirt. The matching suit jacket was draped casually over the back of a chair, and Margo's fingers reached toward the cool, crisp linen.

This is how my real mother would dress, she thought. *Alice Wakefield is my destiny.*

"Hi, sweetheart," Alice said, turning around to give her a smile.

Margo cleared her throat. "Hi, Mom!" she said. *Pure ecstasy.*

Alice's blond hair was the same color as Margo's. Her eyes were the same shade of blue. Her figure was slim and lovely. Everything about her was absolutely, positively perfect. Margo was transfixed.

"Are you OK, Elizabeth?" Mrs. Wakefield asked, cocking her head at Margo.

Margo smiled slowly. "Perfect," she replied, almost in a whisper. She stepped slowly toward her new mother and embraced her tightly.

Mrs. Wakefield seemed surprised, but returned the hug.

"Darling, what's the matter?" she asked.

"Nothing," Margo said, shaking her head. "Everything's perfect." She was still smiling as she hurried out the door, leaving Alice Wakefield staring after her.

❖   ❖   ❖

Alice stood near the open refrigerator, watching the kitchen doorway as if she expected Elizabeth to suddenly reappear.

That was odd, she thought. A hug from her daughter wasn't that unusual. But Elizabeth had seemed so different—almost disoriented.

Of course, Elizabeth and Jessica were having problems again, she reminded herself. She'd heard them arguing in Jessica's room early that morning. Neither of the twins had wanted to discuss it later, but something was obviously wrong, just when it was beginning to look as if all would be forgiven.

Alice sighed. She turned back to the refrigerator and reached for a stalk of broccoli that might or might not be too old to serve for dinner that night. She should have told Jessica to pick up some more at the grocery store.

"There it is!" exclaimed Elizabeth, running into the room. She reached past her mother and grabbed her purse from the counter. She hurriedly tucked her blouse into her gray slacks, and then whirled back toward the door.

"Elizabeth, are you all right?" Mrs. Wakefield asked. "You seemed upset a few minutes ago. And why did you change your clothes? You looked so pretty and spring-like before, in that pink top."

Elizabeth stared at her mother. "Mom, I'm fine," she said. "It's you that I'm beginning to worry about. I haven't seen you since breakfast. And I've been wearing these clothes all day."

She threw her mother one last look, and headed out the door.

Margo sighed in frustration at the wheel of the green Volvo. She could see Elizabeth on her bicycle, growing smaller by the minute as she rounded a corner up ahead. But Margo couldn't follow—not until the toothless old idiot in the station wagon in front of her learned how to drive.

Hot-wiring the Volvo had been easy. But she would lose Elizabeth if the geezer didn't step on it.

"They shouldn't let old people drive cars!" she screamed, pounding her fists on the steering wheel. "I'd like to strangle him with his seat belt!" Margo briefly considered the notion, savoring the thought. Then she shook her head. She had more important things to attend to.

A gleaming, well-sharpened butcher knife was lying beside her on the seat. Margo squeezed the handle, as if for strength. Then she gunned the gas pedal and careened around the station wagon. She laughed at the surprised face of the elderly man in her rearview mirror.

Margo turned onto Country Club Drive.

"There she is!" she exclaimed, catching sight of Elizabeth up ahead, pedaling furiously on her bicycle. "But where is she going in such a hurry?"

Elizabeth coasted up the circular driveway of a stately, brick-fronted mansion with massive pillars. She dismounted, leaned her bike against a tree, and began walking resolutely toward the door.

Margo drove past the house and around the next corner. She parked the car near the curb and took a minute to study the neighborhood. "Good," she said aloud. "There's no one around."

She jumped out, clutching the knife in one hand, and slowly made her way back to the mansion with the white pillars. She ducked behind a bush at the edge of the driveway and peered out.

"That's odd," she whispered. "Why doesn't she go in?"

Elizabeth was sitting on the doorstep, wearing a white blouse and drab gray pants. Elizabeth's taste in clothes was a little too conservative, Margo decided. She fingered the sharp edge of the knife. *I'll make a much better Elizabeth Wakefield than she ever did!*

Elizabeth nervously twisted a lock of her golden hair as she looked up and down the street. She was obviously waiting for someone.

"But who?" Margo whispered to the voice that never really left her.

Patience, came the reply. *Patience.*

Elizabeth twisted a lock of her hair with one finger as she slumped against one of the heavy white pillars of the Wilkins home. In the other hand, she held Todd's letter. *Where can he be?*

A possible explanation kept forcing itself forward in her mind, but Elizabeth shoved it back, unwilling to even consider the possibility. *Todd couldn't have a date with another girl. He just couldn't.*

Since reading Todd's letter the night before, Elizabeth had been desperate to see him, to make up for all the time they had spent misreading each other. Todd had been out of school all day at a basketball tournament. But the basketball game must have ended two hours ago. Where was Todd?

Elizabeth bit her lip and pressed her back against the coolness of the heavy pillar. Then she sat up straight. A black BMW had wheeled into view and was heading up the driveway.

For Elizabeth, the next two minutes seemed to glide by in slow motion. The BMW pulled to a halt. After what felt like an hour, Todd eased himself out of the driver's seat and straightened to his full height of just over six feet. At the same time, Elizabeth slowly rose to her feet, bracing herself against the pillar.

Todd swung the car door shut with one tanned, muscular arm and then swept his dark hair out of his eyes. Then he turned toward the house and noticed Elizabeth standing just a few feet away. Todd froze, his brown eyes wide with surprise, fear . . . and hope.

Elizabeth gazed back at him in silence and longing.

After a minute, Todd opened his mouth. "I . . . I was at Winston's," he said. "I hope you weren't waiting too long."

Elizabeth realized that she'd been holding her breath. She let it out in a long sigh.

"Too long," she answered, holding out the letter. "Too, too long."

Todd recognized the piece of paper in her hand and then looked back at her face, questioning.

Elizabeth took a step forward, put her arms around him, and kissed him—a long, passionate kiss that said everything she wanted to tell him and couldn't find the words for. For the first time in weeks, Elizabeth knew without a doubt that everything was going to be all right.

❖   ❖   ❖

"Face it, Winston," Amy said, reaching out a hand to keep the baby from rolling off the Egberts' dining-room table. "You couldn't change a diaper if your life depended on it."

Winston craned his neck to look around the doorway into the kitchen, where Maria and Lila were heating up a bottle of formula. Apparently, Amy had decided it would be more amusing to stay in here and watch him make a fool of himself.

At least the rest of the coven has gone home, Winston thought gratefully. He sighed and turned his attention back to the baby.

"So I'm no Mother Goose," he admitted, holding up the clean diaper and turning it over and over in consternation.

"More like Donald Duck," Amy said, pushing Winston aside. She pulled out a fresh diaper, expertly wrapped it around Daisy's kicking legs, and then shoved the perfectly diapered baby into his arms.

"How did you do that?" Winston asked, astonished.

"It doesn't take a genius-level IQ," Amy replied.

"Well, obviously not, if *you* can do it."

Amy cast Winston a dark look. "I was about to show you how, but now I don't think I will. And if you're too dense to have figured out how to get the diaper on her by now, Winston, I don't think you ever will."

"Would you like to place a wager on that?"

"What did you have in mind?"

"I'll become an expert diaperer by Friday—as good as you are. And when I win, I get to decide what you'll wear to Olivia's costume party Saturday."

"Okay, you're on," said Amy. "And when *I* win, *you* have to dress up as whatever *I* say for Olivia's party."

"It's a deal," Winston said. "Did you hear that, Daisy? What are we going to make the overconfident Ms. Sutton wear to the costume party? What about Tad Johnson's sweaty football uniform?"

Amy's nose wrinkled. "And you'll look cute, wearing a diaper to match Daisy's. That is, *if* you can get it to stay on," she added, smiling wickedly.

"One more thing," Winston said, with a glance toward the kitchen door. "The bet has to be a secret. It'll be more fun if it's a surprise to everyone when you come with your head shaved, as Chrome Dome Cooper."

Amy scowled. "I wonder what you'd look like in my cheerleading uniform. . . ."

"How romantic," Margo commented to her reflection in the mirror. She remembered every detail of the way Elizabeth's arms had encircled Todd's broad shoulders in the Wilkinses' front yard, and the way his face had slowly lowered to meet hers in a long, tender kiss. Margo sighed.

"They're so much in love," she sighed, "even if she doesn't deserve him as much as I do."

She laughed excitedly. "What a gorgeous boyfriend I have."

She twirled around the small apartment with her eyes closed. "I have the perfect boyfriend, the perfect mother, the perfect house, and the perfect life!" she chirped. "It's everything I've ever wanted. Everything I've been waiting for all these years."

Then the pounding started up again in Margo's head, throbbing, red and intense, against her temples. She clenched her teeth. This was a test, she knew. After a minute, the headache grew less intense, and Margo realized that she had triumphed. After waiting and planning for so long, she *would* triumph.

She leaned toward the mirror and peered deep into her turquoise eyes . . . Elizabeth's eyes.

"Too long," she said softly, in a dead-on

impression of Elizabeth's voice. "Too, too long."

It won't be too long now, said the raspy voice in her head.

Margo smiled, staring at the sharp knife she'd slipped out of the Wakefield kitchen. Perhaps it would come in handy. The knife lay before her on the dresser, its shiny twin reflected in the cracked mirror.

Margo's headache was gone.

Chapter 7

"You're early for school today, Winston," said Mr. Cooper, stopping him in the hallway the next morning. "I trust you're feeling better." He smiled disdainfully. "I heard you were . . . *ill*."

"Um, hello, Mr. Cooper," Winston said, switching his partly opened duffel bag from his right to his left hand, away from the principal. The bag's occupant squirmed sleepily against his leg for a moment and then was still.

Uh-oh, Winston thought desperately. He didn't think Chrome Dome Cooper was particularly bright. If the principal was onto him, then the whole school must know.

"What a shame that you came down with a stomach flu this week, Winston, while your parents are out of town," the principal continued.

101

At least, the principal didn't seem to know about Daisy, Winston thought with relief. *He just thinks I've spent the last few days lying on the beach.*

Winston urgently tried to send a telepathic message to the duffel bag. *Don't wake up, Daisy,* he begged. *Don't blow it for us now.*

"Thank you, sir," he said aloud. "But I'm feeling much better today."

A small, chubby hand had just poked through the open zipper of the duffel bag. Suddenly, Winston really did feel sick to his stomach.

Winston restrained the urge to reach down and shove the tiny fingers back into the canvas bag. If he looked toward the bag, he would risk drawing the principal's attention.

"I'm glad to hear you're well," said the principal. "But I'm still concerned about your health. In fact, I think I will personally call your parents when they return, to ensure that you are truly over your illness."

"Thank you, sir," he said, nearly choking.

Then Daisy gurgled.

Winston gulped.

Mr. Cooper's rather large forehead crinkled. "What was that?" he asked.

"What was what?"

"I heard a noise. It was sort of a gurg— There it is again!"

Winston smiled weakly. "Uh, sorry, sir," he said, trying to force a laugh. "That was my stomach growling. I haven't been able to eat much for the last couple of days, with this stomach flu. I guess I'm kind of hungry."

"Dah-dee!" said Daisy.

"Maria!" Winston called suddenly, desperate to cover the baby's chatter. He reached out to grab his girlfriend by the shoulder as she walked by. He gestured with the duffel bag. "I've got your, uh, things here, Maria!"

"What things?" asked Maria, confused. "Oh, hello, Mr. Cooper."

"It's your, um, softball stuff," said Winston, placing the duffel bag straps in her hand. Maria reached down to see what was in the bag.

"No!" Winston said loudly. "Don't look in there now! I mean, you'll be late. You'd better, uh, take it to the *Oracle* office, like we talked about."

"Winston, I don't play softball!"

Winston laughed. "She's such a kidder," he said to Mr. Cooper. Then he had another brainstorm. "Actually, she's right," he said. "She doesn't *play*. She coaches a *Daisy League* team for little girls. The *Daisy League* stuff is in the bag."

Maria's eyes widened.

"Dah-dee," Daisy announced.

Maria coughed loudly. "Right, Win," she said. "Well, I'll see you in the *Oracle* office, and we can talk about the, uh, game plan. Bye, Mr. Cooper."

She scurried down the hall, carrying the duffel bag.

Winston sighed. Mr. Cooper would have to be an idiot not to know that something was up.

But the principal seemed distracted. He sniffed the air suspiciously. "What is that smell?" he asked. "I'd better talk to the janitor right away about a possible plumbing problem."

Mr. Cooper hurried away, still sniffing.

Winston leaned against his locker, closed his eyes, and banged his head three times against the metal door. Raising a child was turning out to be a lot more complicated than he'd imagined.

Maria sidled into the school newspaper office, holding the duffel bag in front of her. She glanced around the room, saw no teachers, and gently laid the bag on the table.

"What's that?" asked Elizabeth, looking up from the computer where she sat editing an interview.

"Daisy," said Maria, reaching into the canvas bag and lifting the smiling baby out of it.

"Goo-boo," Daisy announced in a serious tone.

"Oh, isn't she darling!" said Penny Ayala, tickling the baby's pink-bootied foot. "Winston asked me to take her for homeroom. I can stay here in the *Oracle* office if I tell Ms. Dalton I'm on deadline. Where's Winston?"

"Mr. Cooper stopped him in the hall," Maria explained.

"What's that smell?" Elizabeth asked.

Before anyone could answer, Winston rushed into the room. He slammed the door and then leaned against it, panting comically.

"Well, Agent 99," he said to Maria. "We've thrown the enemy agent off the track. I see you got the secret weapon here safely."

He stalked toward her and the baby, and then whirled on his heel to point a finger at Penny. "Your mission," he began, "should you choose to accept it, is to keep the secret weapon away from enemy eyes for the duration of homeroom period."

"And if I *don't* choose to accept it?"

"Then I will have no choice but to self-destruct within thirty seconds," said Winston, checking his watch. "And that would make a nasty mess all over your nice, clean newspaper office."

"Okay, I accept!" said Penny, holding up a

hand. "But only if you change her diaper first."

Winston took the baby, laid her on a nearby desk, and began clumsily prying the tapes off the disposable diaper. Maria scrambled in the duffel bag for a moment before handing him a clean diaper, baby wipes, and talcum powder.

Suddenly, the door swung open and Roger Collins's head appeared.

In an instant, Elizabeth, Penny, and Maria all jumped in front of the desk where Daisy lay. Winston stood up quickly behind them, dropping the dirty diaper on the floor and shoving it under the desk with his foot.

"Have any of you seen Paul Jeffries?" asked the newspaper sponsor, from the doorway. "I need to talk to him about covering the district soccer finals."

"Paul hasn't been here this morning," said Penny, lounging to one side in an effort to block the bottle of talcum powder from the teacher's view.

"I haven't seen Paul either," said Elizabeth, leaning across the desk. "But if he stops by, I'll let him know you were looking for him, Mr. Collins."

"Thanks, Liz," said the English teacher, with a skeptical look. He started to back out of the room, but then stopped and checked his watch.

"Shouldn't all of you be heading to homeroom?"

Daisy began cooing, and Winston coughed loudly to cover the sound.

"Winston," said the teacher. "I'd heard you were sick. You really should take care of that cough."

Maria pressed her lips together tightly to keep from laughing. Winston elbowed her in the back.

"I will, Mr. Collins," he promised.

Mr. Collins sniffed. "Does anyone smell something—ah, unusual?" he asked.

"Mr. Cooper thought there might be a problem with the plumbing," Winston explained quickly.

"I see," said Mr. Collins. He scanned the room once more. Then he left the office, shaking his head as he closed the door behind him.

"Goo-boo!" Daisy called after him.

Elizabeth sighed loudly, but Winston and Maria erupted in laughter.

"I don't know what's so funny," Penny said. "We all could have gotten into a lot of trouble if Mr. Collins had seen her."

"I doubt it," Maria said seriously. "I mean, there isn't a rule against bringing your neighbor's baby to school, is there?"

"Maybe not," Penny acknowledged. "But I

still don't think they'd let us keep her here."

"Mr. Collins is too smart not to know that something's going on," Elizabeth warned. "Winston, I'm still not sure that keeping Daisy a secret from the faculty is the best idea. It's not even homeroom yet, and you've already had two close calls. Do you really think you can pull this off for a whole day?"

"I hope so," said Winston, slowly taping a clean, new diaper around Daisy. He grinned and then lapsed into baby talk. "You wouldn't want dis adorable widdle baby to get in trouble with big, bad Mr. Cooper, would you?"

"She *is* awfully cute," Penny agreed.

Winston held up one of Daisy's hands. "Look at this, you guys," he said. "See how teensy-weensy her fingernails are. And you wouldn't believe how soft the soles of her feet are—like little velvet cushions. Isn't she great?"

Elizabeth smiled. "The proud papa, eh?"

"Just wait until your turn comes to watch her, Liz," Winston said, beaming. "You'll fall in love with her, too. Remember, you've got Daisy duty right before lunchtime."

"I'm still not sure about all this," Elizabeth said. "What if there's an accident? What if Daisy gets sick?"

"Liz is right, Winston," said Penny. "You

ought to let the city social services department know about this."

"Social Services would only take Daisy away," Winston protested. "And who knows where she'd wind up—with some psycho, maybe. . . ." He shook his head. "I can't do that to her. If Daisy's mom doesn't come back soon, I may have to turn her over to the authorities. But not yet."

Penny and Elizabeth looked at each other. "All right, Winston," Penny said finally. "We're still with you. But if Daisy's mother hasn't shown up by this weekend, we may not be able to keep your secret any longer."

Elizabeth imagined how Winston had spent every spare moment of the last few days changing diapers and warming bottles. "You know, Winston," she said. "At the very least, this fatherhood thing will wreck your social life."

"Are you kidding?" Winston said wryly. "I've never been surrounded by so many girls in all my life!"

Then a bell rang.

"Rats!" cried Winston. "We're late for homeroom."

"Come on, Daddy," Maria urged. "Hand the baby over to Penny, so we can get out of here."

"Dah-dee," said Daisy, poking at Winston's glasses with a chubby finger.

"No," he said, wagging his own finger back at her. "Me no Daddy." He tapped his chest. "Me Win-ston," he said. "Say Winston, Daisy."

"Dah-dee goo-boo bah-bah?" said Daisy.

He playfully mussed her fine, blond hair. "I guess that's close enough," he said, handing her to Penny.

Maria began pulling Winston toward the door. "You'll take good care of her?" he asked Penny uncertainly.

"Of course I will," she assured him. "You said you trusted me."

"I do," said Winston. He turned to follow Maria, but then stopped. "You'll play with her, Penny? And pay a lot of attention to her?"

"Yes, Winston." Penny sighed.

Winston reached the door and then spun around again. "And you won't let any teachers see her?"

"Of course not!"

Maria pushed Winston ahead of her, out of the room.

A moment later, his head reappeared at the door. "There's plenty of juice and extra formula in the bag, Penny, and some disposable diapers, and Daisy's favorite giraffe. And make sure you keep track of her pacifier. She likes to throw it across the room—"

Maria grabbed Winston's shoulder and

dragged him away. The door swung shut behind them.

"Goo-boo," declared Daisy.

Lila looked at her diamond-rimmed watch, sighed loudly, and began tapping her foot on the pathway in the school courtyard.

Maria finally arrived, breathless, and carefully placed the straps of an open canvas duffel bag across Lila's hand.

"Sorry I'm late," she said. "Daisy's diaper needed changing. I figured you'd rather have *me* do it."

"You figured right," Lila said, identifying the squirming weight in the canvas bag. "Changing diapers is *not* part of my agreement with Winston."

"You're a great humanitarian, Lila," Maria said.

"Don't say things like that in public," Lila protested. "Somebody might hear you. But why is the baby in a duffel bag?"

"What did you expect, a bassinet?" asked Maria. "Winston thought this would be inconspicuous."

"Inconspicuous?" asked Lila, incredulous. "*Me*, carrying something as tacky as a *duffel bag*? And you don't think anybody will notice?"

"Nobody will notice a thing," Maria assured her. "I hid Daisy under one of my cheerleading pompoms a few minutes ago. Coach Horner didn't know the difference!"

"I hope you're right," Lila said skeptically. "I'm not sure which would be worse for my reputation—having people see me with a duffel bag, or with a baby."

"You agreed to do this, Lila."

"I know," Lila admitted. "She was so cute the other day that I couldn't resist. And Winston can be pretty persistent."

"Don't I know it!" Maria agreed. "But aren't you supposed to be in French class this period?"

"Yeah, but Winston couldn't find anyone else and I was happy to get out of a quiz on irregular verbs. So I told Winston I'd watch Daisy, and I told Ms. Dalton I had a dentist appointment!"

"Don't you need a note from home for that?"

"I've got one," Lila said, whipping it out of her pocket. "I told my father I had a dentist appointment, and he signed it, no questions asked."

"I don't know how you do it," Maria marveled. "I'd never have the nerve. . . . Well, Daisy's in the bag, along with a few toys and some bottles and diapers. If you're lucky, nobody will see you, Daisy, or the duffel bag." She gestured around at the deserted courtyard. "There certainly doesn't seem to be anyone out here to notice."

"Who gets Daisy next?" Lila asked.

"Elizabeth will be by for her at the end of the period," Maria told her. "Well, I've got to go. If I'm not cutting up frogs in biology class in about three seconds, Mr. Archer will dissect *me!*"

When Maria was gone, Lila stepped behind a bench into a grassy, sheltered spot rimmed by hedges. She arranged the baby on a blanket on the grass.

"Bah-po?" asked Daisy.

"That kind of talk won't get you anywhere, Daisy," Lila said. "Let's teach you the things every girl needs to know. Here—try this one: 'Put it on Dad's credit card.' Can you say that, Daisy?"

Daisy cocked her head quizzically.

"No, I suppose you can't," Lila acknowledged. "Let's try something shorter: 'Charge it.' Can you say 'Charge it'?"

As Lila leaned forward, Daisy reached up and grabbed a handful of her long, straight hair. She pulled it, hard.

"You little urchin!" screamed Lila, prying the little fist loose.

Daisy looked stricken at her sharp tone, and

Lila's heart went out to the baby. Lila remembered how lonely and confusing her childhood had been, growing up without a mother. She had been lucky enough to get her mother back recently; now her parents were remarried and her life was practically perfect. What if little Daisy weren't so lucky?

The baby gazed up at her with a silent frown. Lila touched her gently on the cheek. "It's OK, Daisy," she said softly. "I didn't mean it."

Daisy smiled broadly, and her tiny tooth sparkled in the sun. "Sha-sha!" she proclaimed, before rolling herself over onto her stomach.

"What did you say, Daisy?" Lila asked. "Did you say 'Charge it'?"

"Sha-sha!" Daisy squealed, excitedly pounding on the blanket with her hands and feet. Lila was impressed at how quickly the squirming motions propelled the baby forward.

"Very good, Daisy. Soon, we'll have you buying out Bibi's swimsuit sale at the mall. Now let's try another word. Can you say 'Porsche'?"

"Miss Fowler?" said a voice from somewhere behind her. Lila whirled around as she jumped to her feet.

Sunlight gleamed off the bald head of the school principal. "I thought I heard your voice," he said. "Why aren't you in class?"

Lila realized that the bench blocked Mr. Cooper's view of Daisy. She skirted the bench and walked toward him quickly. "Mr. Cooper," Lila greeted him. "How nice it is to see you." Lila prided herself on keeping her cool no matter what.

"Where are you supposed to be right now, Lila?" asked the principal, a little more kindly.

"I'm sorry, Mr. Cooper," she said, smiling sweetly and thinking fast. "I'm scheduled to be in French class this period, but Ms. Dalton excused me for a dentist appointment."

"Then why aren't you at the dentist?"

"Actually, I just returned from my appointment a minute ago. I wanted to go to French class, of course, but it wouldn't have been polite to walk in and disturb my classmates in the middle of a quiz. So I came out here to take advantage of the quiet time to do some extra reading for English class next period."

"I assume you have the necessary paperwork to back up your story?" Mr. Cooper said. But Lila could tell that he wasn't suspicious of her anymore. He was just following the rules.

"Certainly, Mr. Cooper," Lila said, dutifully handing over the note from her father and the hall pass from Ms. Dalton.

The principal gave the papers a cursory

glance and handed them back to Lila. "One more thing, Miss Fowler. To whom were you speaking a few minutes ago?"

"Uh, nobody, Mr. Cooper. We're reading Shakespeare in English class. You have to read the lines aloud to really appreciate the language."

"Just be sure to make it to your third-period class when the bell rings, please." He turned away from Lila to walk back toward the school building.

As soon as he was out of sight, Lila darted around the bench to the blanket on the grass.

Daisy was gone.

Lila was annoyed. Where could the little squirt have scooted off to, so quickly? Lila began walking slowly around the perimeter of the courtyard, peering under bushes and benches.

Suddenly, she saw Daisy, about twenty feet away. The baby was lying on her stomach, beneath a bench. She was facing away from Lila, but Lila could see her calmly reaching between a pair of large, expensive tennis shoes to pull on their long, white laces.

The occupant of the tennis shoes, Bruce Patman, sat on the bench with his back to Lila, oblivious to both her and the baby. No doubt, Lila figured, Bruce was cutting class to work on his tan. He wore a portable compact-disc player attached to headphones. Lila could see him beating on the side of the bench with a pair of imaginary drumsticks.

Bruce may have been one of the best-looking guys around, and the richest, but he was not one of Lila's favorite people—to say the least. And she would never live it down if Bruce saw her taking care of a baby. She had to get Daisy away without attracting his attention.

Lila slowly lowered herself to her knees, her eyes on the baby. Daisy murmured something that sounded like "po-sha," but Bruce kept on drumming, oblivious. *Good,* Lila thought. If Bruce's music was loud enough to drown out Daisy's voice, then it would drown out the sounds of Lila's approach, as well.

"Daisy," Lila called, just above a whisper. "Come to Lila."

Daisy scooted her body around to look at Lila, and grinned widely. "Po-shaaa!" she said, wriggling excitedly.

"Winston's right," said Lila, inching forward on her knees. "You *are* a smart baby. Not only did you learn to say Porsche, but you even managed to find the only person around who owns one."

"Teen-age waste-land!" Bruce sang aloud,

emphasizing every syllable with wild strums on an air guitar.

Daisy rocked her body as if she were dancing to the music. Lila was almost within reach of her now, and Bruce's music was so loud that she could hear the tinny-sounding chorus seeping out of his headphones.

Daisy scooped up a handful of dirt and happily ate it. Lila grasped her under the arms and dragged her out from under the bench. Then she put a finger to her mouth. "Shhhh!" she cautioned, nodding toward Bruce, who sat directly in front of them.

Daisy smiled. With one small fist, she made a grabbing motion toward Bruce's dark hair, but Lila pulled her away before she could reach it. Bruce, lost in the song's final guitar licks, didn't notice a thing as Lila tiptoed away.

Lila stopped when she reached the trees on the other side of the courtyard. As she glanced over her shoulder, Bruce stood up, stepped forward, and tripped over his untied shoelaces.

Elizabeth crossed the school courtyard, shaking her head. Why had she told Winston she would watch the baby for him? She could think of a dozen things she could be doing with her study-hall period.

"Liz, you're too nice," she told herself aloud. "You've got to stop agreeing to help everyone in town out of their problems."

She reluctantly stepped off the path at the point where Maria had told her Lila would be waiting with Daisy. Sure enough, there was Lila, sitting under a tree in a grassy spot that was secluded from the main path.

"Where's Daisy?" she asked. Then she stopped short. "What happened to you, Lila? Your jeans are filthy!"

"Don't remind me," Lila warned.

"You look like you've been crawling around on the ground."

Lila rolled her eyes. "Daisy and I had a little adventure," she explained dryly. "Wait until you see what *her* clothes look like."

"Where is she?"

Lila pointed toward the open duffel bag. "In there. Asleep, thank goodness."

"Wait a minute!" Elizabeth called as Lila rose to her feet. "Is there anything I should know about? Will she wake up soon?"

"What do I look like, Dr. Spock? I don't know when she'll wake up. But when she does, you'll want to change her clothes and give her a bottle. There's a clean playsuit in the bag."

She walked a few steps farther before turning

around to impart one last piece of advice. "And keep a close eye on her. She's a lot faster than she looks."

Elizabeth parted the top of the duffel bag and looked inside.

"Goo-boo,". said Daisy, wide awake. On her face was a dab of mud and an adorable smile. On her playsuit was a thoroughly smeared-in layer of dirt and grass stains.

"Oh, Daisy," Elizabeth sighed, shaking her head. "What am I supposed to do with you? I don't know anything about babies."

"Po-shaaa!" Daisy exclaimed, as if she'd just learned a new word. Elizabeth couldn't help laughing. The baby was talking nonsense syllables, but she looked so pleased with herself. Elizabeth lifted Daisy out of the canvas bag, placed her on a blanket Lila had left on the ground, and rooted around in the bag until she found the clean playsuit.

When Daisy was relatively clean, Elizabeth held the warm, soft baby in her arms and carefully placed the baby bottle in her mouth.

"Here you go, Daisy. Drink your apple juice."

Daisy latched on to the bottle with her pink lips and began drinking greedily.

"You are the cutest little baby I've ever seen," Elizabeth whispered.

Daisy's big blue eyes gazed up at her with a look of total trust and adoration. After a few minutes, she'd had enough juice and gently nudged the bottle out of her way.

"Goo-boo," she murmured sleepily, curling the tiny fingers of one hand around Elizabeth's left index finger. As Daisy's eyes closed, a dreamy smile played around the corners of her little mouth. Her perfect eyelashes fluttered slightly, as though blown by her own deep, baby-scented breaths.

Elizabeth cuddled Daisy, enchanted, and leaned forward to kiss her lightly on the forehead.

"I wish I could hold you like this all day!" Elizabeth whispered to the sleeping child. "How could Winston even think about giving you over to strangers?"

Jessica poked at her school lunch with a fork. Salisbury steak—yuck. It was a good thing she didn't feel much like eating. She hadn't felt like eating since the morning before, when Elizabeth woke her up, shaking Todd's letter at her.

Well, if Elizabeth could get along without Jessica, she told herself, then Jessica could get along without Elizabeth. She wouldn't even think about Elizabeth, she decided. Instead, she steered her attention back to the conversation going on around her at the lunch table.

"—and you should have seen the satisfied look on that baby's face when Bruce fell flat on his face!" Lila was saying.

Annie Whitman howled with laughter. "I had no idea Daisy was such a good judge of character! She sure picked the right person to make a fool out of. I wish I'd been there."

"Believe me," Lila confided, pulling from her lunch bag a plastic container filled with sushi. "Bruce Patman needs no help in making a fool out of himself. Bu⁺ Daisy's getting awfully good practice for when she's a teenager. It's important to know how to get men to fall at your feet."

"Daisy sure has *Winston* falling at her feet," Annie replied. "It's nice to see a guy so concerned about a baby." She took a sip of diet soda before continuing. "And he's even getting pretty good at changing all those diapers!"

"Don't remind me," Amy moaned.

"If you ask me, Winston's being a little weird about this whole thing," Lila said. "Don't you think it's wimpy for a boy to be taking care of a baby?"

"No!" Annie objected. "Women are stuck with way too much of the responsibility for raising kids. Wouldn't you want your husband to help out?"

"I'm sure the nanny could do a perfectly good

job without him," Lila answered.

Her tone was smug, but Jessica noticed a flash of pain in her brown eyes. Jessica supposed Lila was thinking of her own childhood. But Lila's parents were back together. Lila's problems were over. *Lila has all the luck*, Jessica thought enviously. She was sure her own problems would have no happy ending.

"Well, Maria doesn't seem to mind," Amy said. "Have you seen the way she watches Winston play with Daisy? You can practically see it in her eyes—she and her hubby Winston pushing the strollers of little Winston Junior and the twins!"

Jessica winced. *Why did Amy have to mention twins?*

"Winston Junior," Lila said with a sniff. "That's a scary thought. I bet the kid would be born with thick glasses and a plaid shirt—"

"And a bad joke for every occasion," Amy finished for her. "You're right. That *is* scary."

"Speaking of men," Annie said, "who did you decide to go to the costume ball with, Lila?"

Lila smiled coyly. "Well," she began, making a big show of counting on her fingers. "Skip Harmon asked me, and so did Michael Schmidt, and Tony Alimenti, and even"—she rolled her eyes—"*Kirk Anderson*."

"Kirk the Jerk?" asked Annie. "What a creep! So which one is it going to be?"

"Tony," Lila answered. "But I haven't given him the good news yet."

"It'll make his day," Amy said. "He's really got it bad for you."

"This costume party is going to be awesome," Lila said. "I haven't met Olivia's new boyfriend, Harry Minton. To tell you the truth, he sounds kind of wacky—the artsy type, like Olivia—but I hear he's got the most gorgeous house in Bridgewater!"

"What time are we getting together at your house on Saturday afternoon?" Amy asked her.

"Oh, I don't know," Lila said, turning to Jessica. "What time do you think you and Elizabeth can make it?"

Jessica dropped her fork with a clatter. "Elizabeth won't be coming Saturday."

Lila looked crestfallen. "What?" she asked. "Why not, Jessica? We were really hoping . . ."

". . . that if we could just get you and Elizabeth together—" Amy began.

"Subtle, Amy," Annie interrupted. "Very subtle."

Jessica squirmed in her chair, sighed loudly, and then gave her friends a wry smile. "Yeah, well, thanks for the thought. But Liz won't come—not if I'm there." She shrugged and sighed again. "Maybe I just won't go."

"No way," said Lila. "You have to come. We're not letting you turn into a hermit."

Amy raised her eyebrows. "Look who's talking. I remember a time when—"

Lila waved a hand to silence her. "That's all over now," she said firmly. "I'm back in action, and happy to be alive again."

Happy to be alive again.

The words echoed in Jessica's head, drowning out the whirl of conversation and laughter in the crowded cafeteria. A sense of unreality overwhelmed her, as if the movement and color of the busy scene were all part of a movie she was watching. Her friends were still talking—something about a shopping trip that evening—but Jessica no longer heard them.

Will I ever again feel happy to be alive? she wondered. She pushed her tray aside and stared at some forgotten student's initials, carved black in the scarred tabletop. But all Jessica could see was her sister's face as it had looked the morning before, with her eyes flashing a cold, blue light.

Chapter 8

"That antique brooch would be perfect to wear with your costume!" Amy exclaimed, admiring the large piece of jewelry Lila was examining at North's Jewelry Store in the mall. "Is that a real ruby?"

"Of course it's a real ruby," Lila said in an annoyed tone, as if there could be any doubt. She tilted the brooch to inspect the tiny, crimson stone.

"I'll bet it costs a fortune," Amy said with a loud sigh. "I'm so broke right now, I can't even afford *fake* jewelry."

"But what about your Cleopatra costume?" Lila asked. "You're going to need jewelry for that."

"I, uh, sort of changed my mind about being Cleopatra," Amy admitted.

"Changed your mind?" Lila asked. "Why? What are you going as instead?"

Amy shook her head. "Believe me, you don't want to know. But I won't be needing any jewelry."

"I don't know what the big secret is. *You* know about *my* costume."

Lila handed the brooch back to the store clerk, along with her father's credit card. Then she turned to Amy again.

"Well, I know how to get it out of you," she said. "How about two scoops of million-dollar mocha at Casey's Ice Cream Parlor? I think we deserve it after all this shopping. Come on, it's my treat."

Josh sat in a corner booth at the mall's ice cream parlor, reading a copy of the *Sweet Valley News*. Nothing in it gave him any clues to Margo's whereabouts. But Georgie's killer was here somewhere; Josh could sense her presence, looming like a storm cloud over this sunny, idyllic town. He was as sure of it as he'd ever been of anything in his life.

Waiting was the worst.

The detective who might be able to tell Josh more about the hit-and-run was out of town until the next week. Until then, Josh's own investigation of the accident was at a standstill.

Josh had spent some time in the library, looking through newspaper accounts of the incident. The victim, the mother of an infant boy, had worked for a prominent local catering firm. The woman had been killed a block from her home. The baby was found in the backseat of the family car, which was still parked in the driveway.

It didn't sound to him like a random accident. Could Margo have been behind the wheel of the car that struck the catering employee? Accidents seemed to happen frequently when Margo was around.

Josh had considered going to the police with his suspicions, but he had no proof—only a gut instinct, fueled by grief, vengeance, and determination. The police here would be no more likely to take him seriously than the officers in Ohio had been about Georgie's case.

He took a long drink of scalding, black coffee, and vowed again that he would find Margo, no matter what. He would get the proof he needed to get the authorities' attention. Or he would take matters into his own hands. Either way, Margo would pay for what she had done.

Suddenly, Josh looked up as a snatch of conversation from the next booth grabbed his attention. A feminine voice had said something about a car accident. Josh held his breath.

". . . ever since the night Sam was killed," concluded a lovely teenage girl with long, blond hair.

Her companion, an elegant, brown-haired beauty, shook her head sadly. "I know, Amy," she said. "Jessica just hasn't been the same since. I thought she and Elizabeth would make up, after that guy came forward and said the accident wasn't Liz's fault. For a while, it looked like things were going to be all right between them."

The blond girl sighed. "I just wish we could get both sisters back together."

Josh slowly exhaled. This was obviously a different accident, probably unconnected with Margo. Still, he reasoned, these girls looked about the same age as Margo. Maybe he should try to get more in touch with what was happening on the high-school scene in Sweet Valley. Maybe that would bring him closer to his quarry.

Of course, Margo had claimed to be in her twenties when Josh's mother had hired her to take care of Georgie. But Josh had never believed her. He was convinced that she was no more than seventeen or eighteen years old, tops. She might be even younger—say, sixteen, like the two attractive girls who were eating ice cream at the next table.

"What about the costume party?" the elegantly dressed brunette asked. "When are you going to tell me what you're wearing?"

"You'll find out soon enough," said the blonde, whose name appeared to be Amy.

"Fine," the other girl said, losing interest. "Be that way. Besides, once I arrive in *my* costume, nobody's going to be paying attention to anyone else on Saturday night!"

"You may have some stiff competition," Amy said. "Everyone who's anyone will be at this party."

Including me, Josh decided suddenly, almost speaking the words out loud. *What better way to find out what's going on in this town?*

A few minutes later, the girls slid out of their booth and left the restaurant. Josh rose slowly, threw a dollar on the table for the coffee, and followed them out.

Josh stepped outside the mall into the twilight. He had lost track of the two girls in the crowded mall, but that didn't matter. He'd be seeing them—and everyone else in town, he hoped—at the costume party Saturday night.

He stopped for a minute and surveyed the bustling parking lot, still lost in thought.

Josh froze. Across the blacktop, under the light of a street lamp, a girl holding a bag from the Lytton & Brown department store was climbing into a black BMW, while a tall, dark-haired boy held the door open. The girl was Margo.

Josh's heart was pounding, his limbs frozen in place. Then he sprang to action, sprinting almost directly in the path of a lime-green Triumph that blared its horn at him impatiently. He had to get to that BMW.

The Triumph careened around him and sped away. Josh stopped, impatiently, and scanned the parking lot again. There it was. The black BMW was heading steadily toward the exit ramp.

Josh ran for a few yards, but the BMW had too much of a head start. It pulled out of the parking lot and disappeared into the steady stream of rush-hour traffic. Josh stopped, panting, and swore under his ragged breath. Then he stood silently and watched the traffic for a full five minutes.

It had to have been Margo, he told himself. Her hair had been long and blond, and she had looked happy and normal—but it was

Margo, all right. Josh would never forget that face.

James wished he could stop thinking about her beautiful, blue-eyed face, but it kept cropping up in his mind, coming between his eyes and the biking magazine he was trying to read Friday morning as he lay on his bed.

"Jessica means nothing to me," James reminded himself out loud, pounding a fist against the mattress. "Nothing except two thousand bucks. She's just a job."

He turned the page roughly and tried to concentrate his attention on an advertisement for a bike. The leather-clad blonde in the photograph had hair just like Jessica's, but she wasn't nearly as pretty as Jessica.

James tossed the magazine aside, rolled onto his back, and stared up at the ceiling. *This is all wrong,* he thought. *She's too young for me. A cheerleader! Not my type at all.*

The phone rang and James lifted the receiver without moving from the bed. "Hello," he said.

"Did you see her last night?" came an intense voice.

"Well, hello, Mandy!" he replied sarcastically. "Yes, this is James. It's so nice to speak with you too."

"I'm not paying you to make small talk with me," she said. "I'm paying you to get close to that goody-two-shoes."

James sighed. This girl might be rude, mysterious, and psychotic, but she was his employer. "Yeah," he said. "We went to a movie and then I took her out for a soda."

"Diet cola, right?" Margo asked with a sneer. "Somebody needs to teach that girl how to drink."

"I think I got most of what you wanted," James said, ignoring the comment. "We talked about tomorrow night's costume party the whole time we were at that burger place. Jessica is really looking forward to it." *And so am I,* he realized with a start.

"What time are you picking her up tonight?" she asked.

"I'm not seeing her tonight," James said. "I'm not seeing her again until the party tomorrow."

"You idiot," Margo said. "You're dating the most popular girl in the junior class. Won't she get suspicious if you don't take her somewhere special on a Friday night? We can't afford to tip her off that you're not for real." Her voice became acid. "If you screw around with my plans, James, I can make your life extremely *painful.*"

She rolled the last word on her tongue as if she were savoring every nuance. James shivered.

"Cripes, Mandy," he said. "Do you always have to be so paranoid? Nobody's messing with your sacred plans."

He was angry—angry at her for being able to make him tense up like this with only a word. If he didn't need the money, he could slam down the phone and never speak to Mandy—or whatever her name was—again. But he did need the money.

"Jessica was the one who broke our date tonight," he told her, modulating his voice. "But she doesn't suspect a thing about me. She wanted to spend time putting her costume together. Besides, she failed a French test this week, and her parents said that if she didn't study tonight, she couldn't go to the party tomorrow."

"Good," Margo said, without a trace of a smile in her voice. "Now tell me about her costume. I want to hear *every detail.*"

James wondered for the hundredth time just what this girl was up to.

"Well?" Margo demanded. "What about the costume?"

James shook his head as if to clear away his doubts. *I'm being an idiot,* he told himself.

Mandy is just some wacko teenager, playing a stupid teenage prank. If a demented girl wanted to pay him good money for an elaborate but harmless prank, who was he to question the details?

But what if Mandy really did intend to harm Jessica?

James opened his mouth to tell her off, but a vision of her cold, turquoise eyes—so much harder than Jessica's almost identical ones—stopped him. Instead, he told her everything she wanted to know about Jessica's costume, in as much detail as he could remember.

But all the while, James wondered just what he was setting Jessica up for.

Margo hung up the phone, jumped off her bed, and whirled in front of the closet.

"What shall Cinderella wear to the ball?" she asked aloud.

The gown James decribed would be easy. All Margo had to do was waltz into Lisette's, pick the same dress off the rack, and tell the salesperson to wrap it up.

As for the accessories, well, it was a good thing Margo had been working on replicating the twins' wardrobe ever since she'd come to Sweet Valley. Except for the dress, Margo was sure she had duplicates of every scrap of clothing that Jessica planned to wear the next night.

She reviewed the list in her head. "A see-through pink scarf—this one ought to do. And I *know* I have a pair of silver pumps like Jessica's—here they are!"

Margo rummaged through a box on the floor of the closet and pulled out a shimmery silk shawl she had bought the week before, to match the one she bought for James to give Jessica. He said she'd be wearing that tomorrow night, too.

"I knew she would!" Margo cried, laughing. "Jessica knows how to manipulate guys. She'll wear the shawl he gave her and the rhinestone earrings he gave her. I knew it from the moment I bought them. I knew she'd think of a costume she could wear them with! I know Jessica Wakefield's mind better than she knows it herself."

Margo's laughter grew to a hysterical pitch as she unfurled the shimmering shawl around her shoulders and twirled across the room, watching its silken folds fan out around her in the mirror.

"Cinderella has found her fairy godmother!" she cried, stopping in front of the mirror and hurling the shawl away from her.

"But one stepsister is enough for anyone."

Behind her, the iridescent silk shawl shimmered in silence as it glided through the air and crumpled, gracefully, on the unmade bed.

Margo whirled around and squinted at the face of the rusty alarm clock across the room.

"I'd better hurry, or I'll be late," she said. Cinderella had to work the afternoon shift at the day-care center.

"I don't know if this is such a good idea, Liz," Winston said over his shoulder.

"What's the harm?" Elizabeth asked him from the back seat of Todd's BMW. "As you said before—all you're going to do is stop by the Project Youth day-care center and ask a few questions."

She checked to make sure that Daisy was still asleep in the car seat beside her. "Remember, Winston, it was your idea to come here after school today."

"What if they try to take her away and put her in an institution?" Winston asked. "I've changed my mind, Todd," he said suddenly. "Turn the car around and take me and Daisy back to my house."

"Elizabeth's right, Winston," Todd told him.

"This is a day-care center, not Social Services. They're not going to steal her away from you. But if Daisy's mother doesn't come back soon, you may have no choice but to go to the authorities."

"I don't get it," Winston said, leaning back into the leather seat. "How could someone leave such a cute little kid behind?"

Elizabeth gazed at the pink and gold baby, sleeping peacefully beside her. "I don't know, Winston," she said helplessly. "You said she had to go to her husband in some Central American country. You can hardly blame her for not wanting to bring an infant along. Maybe they got held up in customs again and just couldn't get out."

"Even Central America has telephones," Winston reminded her. "Why wouldn't she call if she got delayed?"

"There's probably a reasonable explanation," Todd said, slowing the car to a stop. "And most likely she'll show up at your doorstep with it tonight. But until that happens, you need the advice of a professional—someone who knows how to take care of a baby."

He backed the BMW into a parking space directly in front of the day-care center. "And here's a place where you can find one"—he read the sign aloud—"'Little Darlings Day Care, a

Project Youth community center.'"

"It's a silly name," Winston complained.

Elizabeth laughed. "If it'll make you feel better, you don't even have to take Daisy in with you. That way, you can rest assured that nobody will snatch her away. Todd and I will stay in the car with her, while you go inside and find someone to explain the situation to."

Winston turned around in his seat. Elizabeth looked as calm and reasonable as she always did. He suddenly felt like a jerk.

"You're right, Liz," he said with a sheepish smile. "I'm overreacting."

"Overreacting?" Todd asked. "Going ballistic is more like it."

"I admit it," Winston said. "I'm hysterical. I'm manic. I'm having hyper-conniption fits. My little red choo-choo has gone chugging around the bend. I'm a basket case. I'm—"

"Stalling for time?" Elizabeth supplied.

"Exactly," Winston said, leaning over the seat back to gaze, sad-eyed, at the baby.

"Goo-ba giggle!" Daisy announced loudly, reaching a tiny hand toward him.

"Gosh, she's brilliant," Winston said. "A chip off the old blockhead."

"You know what she just said, don't you?" Todd asked.

"What?"

"She said, 'Get inside that day-care center, Blockhead, or I'm going to call Sweet Valley Gossip Queen Caroline Pearce and tell her all about how you tried my pacifier yourself to see why I like it so much.'"

"You did what?" Elizabeth screamed with laughter.

"Right, chief," Winston said quickly. He opened the car door and jumped out. "Synchronize watches. If I'm not back in fifteen minutes, send in the Marines—or the L.A. Laker Girls."

"I know you're on your break, Marla," said Mrs. Waverly, walking into the front office of the day-care center. "But I must run out to the bank. Would you mind taking care of any walk-ins while I'm gone?"

"No problem, Mrs. Waverly," Margo said sweetly. Her boss bustled out the back door just as a skinny teenage boy hesitated in the doorway.

"Yes?" Margo asked suspiciously. Something about the boy looked familiar. Margo didn't think anyone could recognize her—she was wearing her dark glasses, heavy makeup, and her big curly wig—but she hated to take any chances.

141

"Good afternoon, miss," the boy said rather self-importantly, poking his thick eyeglasses back into place.

"Can I help you?" she asked, trying to hide her annoyance.

"Uh, yes," the boy stammered. "My name is Winston Egbert, and I'm looking for some advice."

"Winston Egbert?" Margo said, too loudly. Suddenly, she knew where she'd seen this boy before. He had been Elizabeth Wakefield's nerdy date at the Fowler wedding. For a moment, Margo was afraid she'd been found out, but she dismissed the idea. Whatever Winston was here for, it didn't have anything to do with Margo.

"Well, there's this baby," Winston said. "Her mother left her with, uh—a friend of mine. It was only supposed to be overnight, but that was five days ago, and the mother hasn't come back, and my friend is getting worried."

"How old is the baby?" Margo asked.

"Eight months. And I was wondering—"

"And who is your friend?"

"Just a friend," Winston answered quickly. "And he's worried that if the mother doesn't come back soon, he'll have to give the baby to the Social Services people. I mean, he's taking good

142

care of Daisy; she wouldn't be better off in an institution. But is it illegal to keep a baby in your house, even if the mother gives her to you?"

"Of course it's not illegal," Margo assured him, though she didn't have the slightest idea. "But you still haven't told me who your friend is."

Winston sighed. "It's me," he admitted, looking at his sneakers. "My parents are out of town this week, and I've been keeping her at my house."

"All by yourself?" asked Margo.

"Mostly by myself, but my friends have been helping out."

"Which friends?" Margo asked.

"Oh, my girlfriend has been wonderful. She brings clean diapers and helps me with the bottles."

"Your girlfriend?"

"Yeah, Maria has been wonderful," Winston repeated, looking confused.

Margo let out her breath slowly. "A baby is a big responsibility for one person, especially a teenage boy. You say you have other friends who've been helping, too?"

Winston nodded. "Elizabeth and Todd are out front with Daisy in the car, right now. I don't know what I'd do without them."

Margo froze. "Elizabeth and Todd?" she choked out.

"Yes," said Winston, wringing his hands, too nervous to have noticed her reaction. Margo was relieved. She'd have to keep better control of her emotions. She stood up and casually began walking toward the window.

"There, in the black BMW," Winston said.

Through the open window of Todd's car, Margo could see Elizabeth Wakefield in the backseat, holding a chubby, blond baby in her arms. Elizabeth's beautiful features, so much like Margo's, were lit up in a radiant smile, while her handsome boyfriend watched from the front seat.

Margo understood the whole scene in one glance. Elizabeth was in love with Daisy, and Todd was in love with Elizabeth. Margo felt rage rising within her. Elizabeth had everything in life. And Margo had nothing.

But not for long, said a voice only Margo could hear.

"Isn't she the greatest baby?" Winston asked, behind her. "I couldn't bear to see her put into some orphanage. Besides, I'm sure her mother will be back any day now."

When he turned to Margo, she saw real panic in his eyes. She could make use of that panic.

"You're probably right," she assured him. "But until then, you're going to need more help than a bunch of high-school kids. After all, what do any of you know about taking care of an eight-month-old baby?"

"Can you help me?" he asked.

"Of course," she said sweetly, turning back to the window to watch Elizabeth cuddling Daisy. "I love kids."

Margo's right hand curled into a fist. "Some baby girls don't get the chance to be loved," she continued. "Some get sent to Social Services, and end up in an orphanage or in foster homes, while other baby girls have everything—a nice house, a brother and a sister, a dog, wonderful parents who love them. . . ."

Margo saw that Winston was staring at her strangely.

"But we won't let Social Services put your Daisy in an orphanage!" she said brightly. "At least not for now," she added, remembering that she was supposed to sound responsible. "If you and your friends have been taking care of her this well for five days, you're probably just as good as any institution."

Winston looked relieved.

"Still, it's too much for you to handle alone," Margo said, walking him to the door. Mrs.

Waverly would be back soon, and Margo didn't want her to hear Winston's story.

"Come see me again soon, Winston," she said. "I'll put together a package of information for you about the kind of diet Daisy should be getting. And call me if you need a baby-sitter— free of charge. As I said, I love kids!"

As Winston walked to the car, Margo hid behind the curtains, her eyes riveted on Elizabeth and Daisy. The pounding headache came on so suddenly that Margo gasped. She steadied herself with one hand against the cool windowpane, and watched Elizabeth gently tuck Daisy back into the car seat. She heard herself whispering in a low, raspy voice that wasn't her own, "It . . . isn't . . . fair."

Winston felt better as he strolled outside. It was a relief to know that he wasn't doing anything illegal by keeping the baby.

The girl in the day-care center really had been helpful, he thought. But there had been something a little strange about her, he had to admit. It was more than her bad makeup job. For one thing, the girl had seemed familiar. And she'd spoken with a kind of intensity that was really creepy, her blue eyes going almost blank when she talked about babies who didn't have anything.

Winston shrugged and jumped into the front seat of Todd's car. He was overreacting again, just as his friends had said.

Still, as the car pulled away from the curb, Winston looked back at the window of the day-care center. He couldn't see her, but he had the distinct feeling that the girl was watching from behind the gently swaying curtains.

Chapter 9

Jessica slid the plastic over the top of her new pale-pink gown. There had been a time when she would have ripped through it to get to a new dress. But now, nothing seemed to matter quite as much as it had in the old days—the days before Sam's death and the twins' estrangement.

There was a knock at the door. "Jessica?" called her mother's voice. "Can I come in?"

"Sure, Mom," she said, tossing the dress onto a chair and forcing her lips into a smile.

"How was Lila's get-together this afternoon?" Alice Wakefield asked, stepping gingerly into the clothing-strewn room.

"It was great!" Jessica said, trying to sound as if she meant it. She wasn't exactly lying, she figured. By most standards, it had been a great time. All her girlfriends had been there, and the Fowler mansion was one of the best party sites in town.

"But you didn't have a very good time," her mother said knowingly.

Jessica didn't meet her eyes. "Mom, I think I'm turning into a boring person. Everyone else at the party was talking about costumes and dates, and there I was, sitting like a lump at the far end of the pool, by myself."

"That doesn't sound like the Jessica I know."

"It's all Elizabeth's fault," Jessica said. "She has no right to be so mad at me, after what she did. . . ."

Her voice trailed off.

"I hope you can put that all aside for tonight at least," Alice said, "and have a really good time at the costume party."

"I hope so, too," Jessica said. Then she grinned and pointed at the gown. "I'd better, after spending so much money on that dress at Lisette's. I'll be collecting Social Security before I finish paying you back that advance on my allowance."

Alice Wakefield lifted the dress off the chair and rubbed the light, filmy fabric between her fingers. "Well, this will make a perfect Cinderella's ball gown. I can't wait to see you in it. How did you ever get James to agree to come as the prince? As I remember, the last time there was a costume party around here, there was some dissension between the female and male sides of the teenage population."

Jessica laughed. "I wanted us to go as Romeo and Juliet, but Sam refused to wear tights!" She bit her lip. "Sometimes I'm afraid that it's wrong of me to go on having a good time, when poor Sam . . . But that's silly. Sam would want me to have as much fun as I can."

"Yes, I think he would," Alice replied. "I know how much he admired that old Jessica Wakefield 'knock 'em dead' party attitude."

"And I'm going to muster it up again tonight," Jessica vowed, "even if it kills me."

Elizabeth pulled the crinoline over her slip and fastened it in place around her waist. Tonight was going to be terrific. *Everything* was going to be terrific, now that she and Todd were back together.

They hadn't had much time to plan their costumes, but it had been surprisingly easy to come up with an idea they both liked. *Surprising, compared to the last costume party they'd attended together,* Elizabeth recalled. She had wanted them to be George and Martha Washington.

Todd had wanted them to go as a horse. *A horse!*

This week there had been no arguments. And they had come up with a pretty good costume idea, Elizabeth decided, even if they wouldn't be the most original pair at the party. What mattered was that she and Todd were together again and were more in love than ever.

Enid, of course, had been thrilled at Elizabeth's and Todd's reunion. Elizabeth only wished that Enid's boyfriend, Hugh, didn't have to go to his cousin's bachelor party that night. She felt bad about leaving Enid without a date for the costume party, after they had planned to go together. Enid had insisted that Elizabeth go with Todd. But Elizabeth was determined to make sure that Enid had a wonderful time, even without a date.

Elizabeth surveyed the neatly arranged toiletry items on the top of her dresser, and then remembered that she had left her hairbrush in the bathroom.

She walked across her bedroom humming, feeling her nyloned feet sinking luxuriously into the soft, off-white carpeting. It was wonderful to be able to appreciate the little comforts of life again, after walking around for so long in a daze of fear, dread, and guilt.

Of course, her relationship with Jessica was

152

still a sore spot. But millions of people had perfectly full lives without a twin sister. Elizabeth could, too. For now, at least, it was easier to cut her losses and concentrate on her relationship with Todd.

She pushed open the bathroom door. At the same time, Jessica opened the door on the opposite side of the bathroom, and entered from her adjoining room.

Elizabeth stopped humming.

Jessica jumped backwards, stunned. For a moment, she thought she'd opened the bathroom door and come face-to-face with her own living, breathing reflection. Of course, it was only Elizabeth.

The same thing had happened to them about a million times before in the bathroom that connected their two rooms. They used to laugh about it. But this time, Elizabeth hardly glanced at her. She reached around Jessica and grabbed a hairbrush off the counter. Then she disappeared back into her own room without a word, closing the bathroom door firmly behind her.

Jessica listened to the loud, hollow-sounding slap of the door as it swung shut between the two sisters, and instantly forgot her resolve to be happy that night.

"How can I be happy when Sam's dead, and I've betrayed my own twin sister—twice?" Jessica whispered to the mirror. Then she sat down, hard, on the edge of the bathtub, covered her face with her hands, and began to cry with silent, wrenching sobs.

Elizabeth stood in the center of her bedroom, still holding the hairbrush. "I will not let this upset me," she whispered.

She sat on her bed with a sigh. She hated the awkwardness between herself and Jessica, but she had thought she was becoming resigned to it. Tonight felt different—eerie, somehow. . . .

Suddenly, Elizabeth knew what was unsettling her. It was a feeling of déjà vu. This was exactly what getting dressed had been like on the night of that awful Jungle Prom. Both twins had desperately wanted to be prom queen. Elizabeth had been so angry at her sister—so sick and tired of giving in to Jessica's every whim. This time, she had told herself, she would not back down.

Their chance meetings in the bathroom the night of the prom had been chilly, with none of the excited chatter they used to share as they pulled on their panty hose and slid into their best dresses in preparation for a Saturday night out.

Elizabeth shuddered. Of course, just because

the night Sam died had begun like this, she had no reason to assume that disaster would strike tonight, as well.

"The bad luck is over," she whispered, thinking of Todd. Elizabeth began humming again as she brushed her long, blond hair, loving the silky feel of it around her bare shoulders. She imagined herself, warm and comfortable, in Todd's strong arms.

Tonight, she would try not to think about Jessica at all.

Jessica had stopped crying but was still sitting on the edge of the bathtub when she heard the knob turn on the door to Elizabeth's room. She jumped up instantly, switched on the faucet, and was splashing her face with cold water when Elizabeth, still wearing only a slip and crinoline, entered the room.

"Oh!" Elizabeth exclaimed, surprised. Then the expression in her eyes hardened and her tone became formal. "I didn't know you were still in here," she said stiffly.

"It's all right," Jessica answered, just as formally, her face dripping. "I was just leaving." She grabbed a towel and quickly left. Once in her room, she closed the door behind her and leaned against it while she furiously dried her face.

Scenes from another Saturday night crowded into Jessica's brain: she and Elizabeth, scowling at each other when they accidentally met in the bathroom as they dressed for the Jungle Prom. . . . Jessica's fury at the dance, when Todd was named king and Elizabeth seemed a shoo-in for queen . . . Jessica's own manicured hand, pouring grain alcohol into Elizabeth's punch to prevent her from winning the title . . . and the scene of the accident, with the Jeep listing crazily to one side and the police pulling Jessica away as she tried frantically to get close enough to see—while the queen's crown, forgotten, lay behind her in the dirt.

If only they were getting ready for *that* dance, instead of this one! If only this were *that* Saturday night, and there was still time to run into Elizabeth's room, wish her the best of luck in her campaign to be prom queen, and cheerfully help her zip up her dress. If only . . .

It was no use. All Jessica could do now was get ready for tonight and try her best to forget about that other night. At least she had James now.

"James!" she said aloud. It must be getting close to seven o'clock, when he was supposed to pick her up. And Jessica hadn't even started to get dressed.

She shook her head and tossed the towel to

the floor. She didn't have Elizabeth anymore to keep her on schedule—well, *almost* on schedule. She sighed as she sat on the bed and began pulling on her new white panty hose that glittered with tiny silver stars.

Jessica threaded Sam's pearl teardrop-shaped earrings through her ears. She had planned to wear the rhinestone earrings James had given her, but she had suddenly changed her mind. Thinking about the Jungle Prom had made her think about Sam, and the pearl earrings made her feel closer to him. She knew James would understand.

Jessica stood back to inspect herself in the mirror. She couldn't help smiling; she was beautiful. Her hair was piled elegantly on top of her head and held in place by shiny gold combs. The ball gown looked as soft as a cloud, tinted the faintest of pinks by the promise of a sunrise. The shawl shimmered on her shoulders with subtle hints of color.

Jessica didn't own a pair of glass slippers, but her silver pumps sparkled like starlight; on a darkened dance floor, they'd be close enough.

She held her filmy pink scarf in front of her eyes, and nodded happily. Good. She could see through it quite easily. Olivia had urged everyone to wear costumes that covered their faces, to add to the air of mystery. The scarf would work well. Jessica pinned it to the gold combs in her hair, so that it fell gently over her face like a bridal veil. The effect was perfect—romantic, yet dramatic. And she could lift the scarf back over her hair if she got tired of seeing the world through its rose-colored folds.

She left it that way now, draped backward over her golden hair. She knew that James was waiting downstairs—her father had called up to both girls a few minutes earlier that their dates had arrived.

She stepped out into the hallway and stopped at the top of the stairs. She could hear Elizabeth's voice downstairs, and she wasn't sure she wanted to run into her again tonight. For a moment, Jessica considered waiting until Elizabeth and Todd had left.

No. Jessica Wakefield wasn't afraid of anything, especially not her own sister. She froze a smile onto her face and advanced regally down the stairs, an arm outstretched to take James's hand.

Then Jessica saw Elizabeth, and gasped.

Elizabeth's silver-clad feet peeped out from under her full, pale-pink ball gown. A shimmering silk shawl cascaded down her shoulders, and a wisp of a pink scarf seemed to float on her elegantly arranged hair.

The girls' parents and dates looked from one twin to the other, speechless.

The twins weren't dressed identically, Jessica realized, but they were awfully close. Elizabeth's dress was a shade darker than Jessica's, and the veil that shimmered in Elizabeth's hair was really more white than pink. Small crystal earrings sparkled in Elizabeth's ears. Still, she could hardly believe how close Elizabeth had come to matching her costume.

"Cinderella?" the sisters asked in unison. They both nodded solemnly.

If this had happened a few months earlier, Jessica knew, the twins would have laughed and hugged each other. But now, Elizabeth took Todd's hand, murmured a few words to her parents, and swept toward the door, her pink gown rustling as she brushed by her sister.

"Have a good time, kids, but don't stay out too late," Mr. Wakefield called after Todd and Elizabeth. Jessica knew he was trying to sound as if nothing awkward had happened.

"Don't worry about a thing," Todd replied, stopping in the doorway. He was speaking to the twins' parents, but looking only at Elizabeth, and Jessica felt a lump in her throat when she saw the love in his deep-brown eyes.

"Are you all right?" James asked.

"Perfect," Jessica said, fixing a broad smile on her face. "And you look absolutely dashing!"

For the first time, she took a good look at his costume, and felt her spirits rise. James was gorgeous. His prince's outfit consisted of navy slacks and a cornflower-blue satin tunic that made his eyes even bluer. His white sash was studded with official-looking medals and ribbons, and his long light-brown hair was swept rakishly to one side.

But James was staring at Jessica, shaking his head as if he'd never seen her before. "And you are dazzling," he said slowly.

Jessica smiled more naturally. Maybe the night wasn't going to be so bad, after all.

Chapter 10

Elizabeth held Todd's hand as they walked under an ivy-covered archway into the garden behind Harry Minton's antebellum-style mansion.

"Olivia's boyfriend really knows how to throw a party!" Todd said, gesturing toward a lattice-work gazebo where a group of musicians played Dixieland jazz.

"This place is breathtaking," Elizabeth said, her eyes wide under the pale, translucent veil. She tossed the veil back over her hair so that she could see the decorations better. Tiny lights twinkled from every surface and every tree, and the sweet smell of flowers mingled with the delicious aromas of spicy hors d'oeuvres.

"Elizabeth!" called Enid, rushing over in an aviator costume. Rosa Jameson, dressed as

161

a witch, was right behind her.

"You look terrific, Enid," Elizabeth said warmly.

"Good evening, Ms. Earhart," Todd greeted her. "What a great idea for a costume!"

"What costume?" Enid asked. "This isn't a costume. I've always been naturally flighty."

"That's not true!" Elizabeth protested. "But you do make a good Amelia Earhart."

"Rosa," began Todd, "haven't I seen that get-up somewhere before?"

"I'll give you a hint," Rosa said, her dark eyes twinkling like the lights strung from the tree branches above her head. "'Double, double toil and trouble!'"

"Aha!" Todd said. "It's your costume from *Macbeth* a few months back."

"Speaking of costumes, you two look terrific," Enid said, appraising Todd and Elizabeth's outfits.

"I still say we should have come as a horse," Todd joked.

Enid turned to Elizabeth. "Is he still neigh-saying your costume ideas?"

Elizabeth grinned. "You know Todd," she said. "His fashion sense needs to be reined in at times, but he's still my mane man."

Rosa rolled her eyes. "I think I'm going to be sick."

"Actually," Enid said, "I think Cinderella and Prince Charming was quite an inspiration."

Elizabeth and Todd glanced at each other.

"As it turns out," Elizabeth said, "it wasn't such an original idea. Jessica will be showing up in a few minutes, wearing a costume almost exactly like this one."

Rosa's eyes widened. "Why would she do that?"

Elizabeth shrugged. "It's possible she didn't know what I was wearing."

"Does it really matter?" Enid asked diplomatically. "There's no reason why you can't have a perfectly good time, no matter what costume Jessica's wearing."

Elizabeth grinned. "You're right," she said. "I won't even think about Jessica or her costume tonight. Though it's kind of strange that I haven't seen her here yet. She was only a few minutes behind us."

Suddenly, Elizabeth felt a chilly breeze stir through the large, dark garden. She wrapped her arms around her. "Is anyone else getting kind of cold?" she asked.

"It seems warm to me," Enid said. "But your shawl's pretty light. Would you like my jacket?" She began to take off her leather aviator's coat.

Elizabeth waved it away. "Oh, no thanks,"

she said. "It was just one little breeze. Don't spoil your costume on my account."

"Speaking of costumes," Rosa said, staring wide-eyed toward the entrance arch, "you'll never believe what just walked in."

Todd whistled as Amy Sutton stomped toward them.

"Don't anybody say a word!" Amy cautioned as she flounced past them, clutching in her fist a fold of her long black skirt to keep it from catching on a rosebush.

The four burst into laughter.

"I wonder what changed her mind about Cleopatra," said Elizabeth. "Who ever thought we'd see it—Amy Sutton dressed as a nun!"

Elizabeth was whirling around the flagstone patio that served as a dance floor, supported by Todd's arms. Everything was as perfect as she'd imagined. The musicians were playing a big-band number. Tiny lights were entwined through the latticework roof over part of the patio, and they twinkled like stars. The smell of Todd's aftershave brought back memories of every wonderful evening they'd ever shared, and Elizabeth couldn't remember ever feeling so much in love with him.

"It's good to see you two back together!" a

voice said behind her. Elizabeth turned and smiled at Olivia, dancing with Harry.

"Mickey and Minnie Mouse sure dance a mean tango!" Harry said, pointing to one of the dancing couples. Does anyone know who they are?"

"That's my brother, Steven, and his girlfriend, Billie," Elizabeth said with a touch of pride.

"Their costumes are really cute," Enid said, "but somebody ought to tell them this isn't a tango!"

"I didn't know you had a brother," Harry said. "I thought all siblings in your family looked exactly alike."

"They do," Todd explained. "Elizabeth left her Mickey Mouse ears at the cleaner's."

Elizabeth ignored him. "Jess and I look just like Mom, but Steve's the spitting image of our father," she explained. She managed to control her voice, but just thinking about Jessica set her nerves on edge. She was still angry with Jessica for hiding Todd's letter, and the duplicate costumes tonight hadn't made her feel any more charitable toward her sister. If there was anything Elizabeth didn't want to think about tonight, it was Jessica.

Todd seemed to sense Elizabeth's mood. He gracefully steered the subject away from the twins. "I'd like to extend my compliments to the host and hostess," he said with a formal salute toward Olivia and Harry. "This is a swinging party."

"Thank you, Prince Charming," Olivia said with an odd, closed-lipped grin. She wore a brownish dress with a square-cut neckline and rows of embroidered trim. Her usually wild brown hair was parted in the middle, and her demure smile held an air of pure mischief. "We're glad you could swing by."

"I get it!" Todd exclaimed suddenly, pointing to the ornate tunic Harry wore and the paint brushes sticking out of his belt. "You're Leonardo da Vinci and the Mona Lisa!"

Harry and Olivia beamed at Todd's recognition and the two couples walked to the edge of the dance floor to where Enid and Rosa were standing.

"So this is where the rest of the exciting people are," Winston Egbert interrupted as he and Maria Santelli joined them. Winston bounced little Daisy in his arms.

"The place looks fantastic!" Maria marveled, tossing a loose strand of orange hair out of her eyes. "You've done a great job with the decorations, Harry," Maria continued. "Or should I say, Leonardo?"

"My loyal model, Mona here, is the real *artiste*. My biggest contribution was that I happen to live in this white elephant."

"Don't listen to him," Olivia said. "He's a lot more artistic than he lets on."

Enid sighed. "The house looks like something out of *Gone with the Wind*."

Elizabeth took another look around the garden at all the wild costumes. She suppressed a shudder. There was something strange about seeing all her friends looking like unfamiliar versions of themselves. Somebody in a mask brushed by her. Elizabeth jumped when she saw a knife sticking out of his chest and dark blood dripping down his shirtfront. She realized an instant later that the knife was plastic and the blood was fake. She exhaled slowly, glad that Todd hadn't noticed her reaction.

"If the house is Tara," he was saying to Maria, "then Lila Fowler's costume is the most appropriate one here."

He pointed across the garden. Lila stood at the refreshment table, resplendent in white ruffles, with a huge, jeweled brooch sparkling at her neck. As Elizabeth's group watched, tall, dark Tony Alimenti—dressed as a Confederate officer—handed her a glass of punch.

Olivia raised her eyebrows. "Lila *is* Scarlett

O'Hara," she admitted. "And what a gorgeous dress! It must have cost her a fortune."

"If I know Lila, she's wearing *hairpins* that cost more than my entire outfit," Enid said. "But you're right about her dress."

"'Frankly, my dear—'" Winston began.

"Actually," Olivia said quickly, gesturing around the garden, "a lot of people helped with the decorations for tonight. The little lights were Robin Wilson's idea."

Elizabeth followed her glance. A mime sat on a wooden bench at the other end of the dance floor, gesturing to a gypsy fortune-teller in what appeared to be sign language. The mime's face was painted white with black crosses over her eyes.

Elizabeth shivered. Mimes had always given her the creeps, for some reason. Maybe it was the way their painted faces couldn't quite hide their real expressions. And this mime struck her as particularly eerie, somehow desperately sad and demonically evil at the same time.

Then the mime began to laugh, and the illusion was gone. It was only Robin Wilson, amused at her failed attempts to communicate in pantomime with the gypsy, who had suddenly become Annie Whitman.

Elizabeth closed her eyes tightly for an instant and scolded herself about letting her imagination run wild. She forced herself to pay attention to the conversation going on around her.

"Did you see Amy Sutton?" Enid asked Maria and Winston, her coppery brown hair glistening unnaturally under the twinkling lights. "There must be a story behind that costume."

Winston shook his head, as if in dismay. "I've been trying to convince Amy to kick the habit! But she's having nun of it."

Todd eyed him suspiciously. "Something tells me you know more than you're saying about Sister Amy's new calling."

"Who, me?" Winston asked. "I'm just the bandleader."

"You three make a lovely family, Win," Elizabeth remarked, trying to sound natural, despite the irrational uneasiness she still felt. "But what are you supposed to be? And what's with Daisy?" she asked, pointing to the black wig perched crookedly on the baby's head.

Winston scowled dramatically. "Daisy?" he asked. He pitched his voice an octave lower than usual and laid on a heavy but unrecognizable accent. "That ees my Leetle Ricky!"

Rosa nodded. "Ahhh! That explains your lounge-lizard shirt! You're Lucy and Ricky Ricardo, with Little Ricky, from the old 'I Love Lucy' re-runs."

Winston shoved the baby at Maria, yanked forward a set of bongo drums that hung from a strap around his neck, and beat on them glee-fully with his palms.

"Baba-loo!" he sang tunelessly.

"Ba-wooo!" Daisy repeated.

Winston laughed and reverted to his normal voice. "I told you she was a chip off the old blockaroo."

"Tell us, Rosa," Enid asked. "You're the resi-dent expert. What does 'baba-loo' really mean in Spanish?"

"Good question," Winston said. "I've been singing 'baba-loo' to everyone all evening. I shouldn't be embarrassed about it, should I?"

"Yes!" said two vaguely familiar voices, in uni-son. Elizabeth saw that they belonged to Tweedle-dum and Tweedle-dee, who were pass-ing by Winston as he spoke. Elizabeth opened her mouth to ask who was under the grinning masks. But the pair was already gone, swallowed up in the colorful, shifting crowd.

"I think it translates as, 'I can't sing worth beans,'" Rosa said.

"Wasn't the baby supposed to be a big se-cret, Win?" Todd asked. "I'm surprised that you would bring her out in public."

"Well, I sure didn't want the teachers to know I had her in school Thursday," Winston said. "But this is my last night as a baby-sitter, so it doesn't matter who sees her now. I don't know about Daisy's parents, but *my* parents are coming home tomorrow. I've got to get her to somebody official before they arrive."

A masked sultan and harem girl glided by on the dance floor. Their costumes gleamed in an unnatural blaze of orange and yellow satin. Again, Elizabeth felt a chill come over her. Something about the combinations of wild, colorful costumes all around her was profoundly frightening.

"Oh, Fred Mertz!" Winston called to the sultan, who suddenly turned into Bruce Patman. "Come hear me sing baba-loo!"

"Ba-wooo," Daisy added firmly.

Bruce began steering his date, Pamela Robertson, toward the far side of the dance floor. "If we pretend we don't know him, maybe he'll go away," Bruce said in a loud stage whisper.

Enid laughed. "Has anyone ever noticed how people run in the other direction when Winston's around?"

"Speaking of running away, I think we're supposed to be mingling," Olivia said, nudging Harry.

171

"There's never any rest for the host!" Harry said with a smile. "Come on, Mona. Or is it Lisa? Let's go be sociable. The rest of you should be ready to put your masks on, if you've taken them off," he added. "The costume judging will start soon, and the winners will be announced sometime after ten thirty."

"Well, I'm running, too," Rosa said. "I will die of starvation if I don't try some of those appetizers within the next two minutes. Anyone want anything? I could eat a horse!"

Todd turned to Elizabeth. "See how popular we'd be if we'd come dressed as a horse?"

"This is getting ridiculous!" Winston complained. "I work my fingers to the bone, doing my best to keep up the title of class clown, and suddenly I'm surrounded by amateurs. These days, everyone's trying to be a comedian!"

"Ba-wooooo!" cried Leetle Ricky, clapping her hands.

Elizabeth walked by herself along a garden path outlined by glowing luminaries.

She turned back toward the dance floor, where Todd was dancing with Enid to a fast rock-and-roll song. Elizabeth had pushed them together, claiming that she wanted to take a better look at the gardens. Todd had seemed reluctant to leave her alone. But Elizabeth knew he would assume that her need for solitude was an excuse for making sure Enid was having fun, too.

Enid did seem to be having fun—so did Todd, Elizabeth noticed approvingly. It was too bad that she, Elizabeth, was feeling too spooked to enjoy a really great party.

Just then a fair-haired boy Elizabeth had never seen before moved onto the dance floor, blocking her view of Todd and Enid. The boy was dressed in a hastily thrown-together Sherlock Holmes outfit—jeans and a T-shirt, but with a hat, cape, pipe, and oversized magnifying glass.

Somehow, the fair-haired boy didn't seem to fit in with the party atmosphere. He was looking away from Elizabeth, but she could see enough of his expression to know that he was frowning.

Elizabeth chastised herself for thinking there was something odd about the fair-haired boy. After all, she herself wasn't smiling or talking to anyone, either. Maybe Sherlock Holmes had come with a friend and didn't know anybody else at the party. Or maybe he just didn't feel sociable tonight. He wouldn't be the only one, Elizabeth reminded herself.

She turned and walked in the opposite direction, down a flagstone path that led in a wide curve around the perimeter of the garden. Ducking under a small, pretty arch, she found herself alone in a separate courtyard, isolated from the main garden by tall boxwood hedges. The music and laughter from the party seemed to recede, as if absorbed by the dark shrubbery.

A gust of wind surprised Elizabeth. She glanced up and stifled a cry. Sharp points of light jerked wildly overhead—as if the black sky, littered with stars, were tilting wildly. She felt as if she was about to lose her balance, and she sat down hard on a stone bench. As she did, the breeze lifted the filmy veil from her hair, and floated it down slowly over her face.

"There's nothing to be afraid of," she told herself aloud. "The stars aren't tilting. It's just those funny little lights moving in the breeze."

She stood up and planted her feet firmly on the flagstone path. Then she took a deep breath, causing the veil to flutter in front of her mouth. She looked around the small courtyard to prove to herself that there was nothing to be afraid of.

A marble fountain spattered limply in the center of the patio, its water glowing an acid green in the strange light. Opposite the pretty entrance arch, two tall boxwood hedges loomed over a dark, narrow passageway into the unlit part of the garden. She hadn't even known it was

174

there until she was almost on top of it.

Elizabeth turned and walked past the fountain and across the courtyard toward the pretty latticework arch where she'd begun. She breathed deeply of the floral-scented air, reminding herself sternly that she wasn't afraid of the dark.

Then she froze. Somebody was standing outside the arch, looking in at her.

The figure stepped forward to face Elizabeth, and she breathed a giddy sigh of relief. The girl's long, full gown was pale pink, and her shoulders were draped with a shimmering shawl exactly like the one Elizabeth was wearing. It was a girl in a Cinderella outfit that was almost identical to Elizabeth's. It was Jessica.

"You scared me, Jess," Elizabeth said, too relieved to remember that she was angry at her sister.

Jessica stared at her for a moment without saying a word. Then she turned and disappeared through the archway in a whirl of pink, her large rhinestone earrings flashing brilliantly as she turned.

Elizabeth inhaled sharply. *Rhinestones?* She was sure she remembered which earrings Jessica had been wearing that evening—the teardrop-shaped pearls that Sam had given her.

Elizabeth ran to the archway to look for her sister. Jessica was nowhere to be seen.

Suddenly, Elizabeth recalled the recurring nightmare that had plagued her in the weeks following the accident. She was standing in the brittle sunlight on the shores of Secca Lake, staring at a girl who looked exactly like Jessica—a girl who moved toward Elizabeth in slow motion, clutching a gleaming butcher knife.

Elizabeth shook herself as if to dissolve the image. Then she lifted the veil from her face and quickly made her way back to the party, crossing her arms tightly in front of her. In the last few minutes, the air in the garden had become much colder.

Josh knew he was getting warmer. He stared intently at the dancers. *Margo is here somewhere.* He could practically taste her presence in the air.

But picking her out might be more difficult than he had anticipated, among all these young people in costumes. The costumes were more elaborate than he had anticipated. In fact, he felt a little underdressed in the Sherlock Holmes outfit he'd thrown together at the last minute. But he hadn't wanted to spend much time or money on it, and the detective seemed like a natural choice.

So far, the costume wasn't giving him much luck. If Margo was here, Josh didn't know where. Which of the dancers could she be?

The gypsy fortune-teller was too tall, he decided quickly. A girl of about the right height was dressed as Amelia Earhart and dancing with a prince or duke or something. Josh's heart began to pound. He wasn't certain, but the prince looked a lot like the boy he'd seen with Margo in the mall parking lot—handsome, tall, and well-built, with dark, wavy hair.

The couple turned and Josh got a glimpse of the aviator's round, pretty face. Even through her heavy flight goggles, Josh could see that she was nothing like Margo.

He exhaled slowly and narrowed his eyes. He would find Margo tonight, he vowed grimly. He would unmask her.

Todd was elated. He loved the feel of Elizabeth's hand on his shoulder as they danced. He loved the way her eyes showed turquoise through the pale wisp of a scarf that partly hid her face. The weeks of their separation had been miserable ones, and he blamed himself for the entire misunderstanding. Todd smiled down at Elizabeth and vowed silently that he would never doubt her again.

"Are you feeling better now?" he murmured into her ear, feeling a twinge of concern about something he'd seen in her face when she had returned from her walk alone in the garden. She had seemed disturbed about something—afraid, actually. But she had insisted that nothing was wrong.

"I'm feeling great," she said now, smiling up at him. "Except that I'm really parched. I think I'll go grab a cold drink. Do you want anything?"

"No, thanks."

"In that case, Todd, Winston looks like he could use some adult company over there. Why don't you give him a hand until I get back?"

She pointed to Winston, who was apparently pleading with a red-faced Daisy to stop crying. Todd laughed and good-naturedly sauntered over to lend a hand.

"Have you seen Maria?" Winston said desperately. "She's supposed to be here to take Daisy for a while." He looked past Todd, and continued. "Speaking of our better halves—"

Todd felt a hand on his shoulder. Elizabeth was back already, looking like a blur of pink gauze as she grabbed his arm, whirled him around, and dragged him onto the dance floor. He waved at Winston and followed her willingly as the band started a slow, romantic song.

The moment Todd turned to face his partner, he realized that he'd been mistaken. It wasn't Elizabeth he was dancing with at all. This had to be Jessica.

Jessica was known for dramatic gestures. They had dated only briefly, while he and Elizabeth were apart, but both of them knew that there was nothing between them. This was probably some sort of peace offering, he figured.

Still, Todd had no idea what he should say to her. After a minute, he realized that it didn't matter. For once, Jessica seemed content with silence. In fact, she hadn't spoken a word.

Todd's eyes widened when he felt Jessica's hand slip from his shoulder and slide around to the middle of his back. He pulled away as far as he could without being impolite, but she swiveled her hips forward to follow the line of his body.

Why was she doing this to him, after everything they'd been through? Todd prayed that the song would end soon.

When Jessica's hands began caressing his back in soft, slow circles, Todd began to feel panicky. He couldn't figure out what had gotten into her. He had known right away that this Cinderella wasn't Elizabeth, but now it hardly seemed like Jessica. She'd always been one of the biggest flirts in town, but he'd never seen her come on to anyone like this—let alone to him.

"Jessica—"

She put a finger to her lips—barely visible beneath the pink scarf that covered her face. Her embrace grew tighter, and Todd was so nervous that he didn't think he could have spoken at all, even if he'd wanted to.

When the song finally ended, Todd ducked out of her arms before the echo of the last note had died down. In his haste to get off the dance floor, he bumped into another couple, mumbled something apologetic, and scrambled away to find Elizabeth. Somebody behind him began making an announcement about the costume contest winners being revealed soon, but Todd barely heard. All he knew was that he had to get away—and that he couldn't look back.

As he ran from Jessica, he felt her intense, cold eyes boring into his back like ice picks.

Margo sighed dreamily. She hated to see her dance with Todd end. It had been so romantic— how lucky she was that a slow song had come along, just when Elizabeth had left Todd to get a drink.

Nothing is luck, said the low, raspy voice in her head.

"Of course," Margo whispered aloud, surprised that she hadn't realized it before. "The stars are helping me tonight."

The stars had come down closer to earth and were hanging all over this party, sitting in the trees and lining the little wooden archways that led party guests from one area of the garden to another. The slow song had not come because of sheer luck. It was part of a plan. Everything was part of the plan.

And soon, the best part of the plan would unfold. Cinderella would become the princess. And Todd would be her prince.

"Jessica!" said a voice behind her. Margo felt a hand on her shoulder. She whirled, groping for the switchblade she wore strapped to her thigh.

Then she saw who it was, and relaxed. Margo recognized the pretty, brown-haired girl from the wedding she'd attended at the Fowler mansion.

"I haven't seen you all night!" said Lila, dragging her off the dance floor. "Where have you been hiding?" A tall, gorgeous boy—Italian, Margo decided—followed Lila with a worshipful look on his face. Someday soon, boys would follow *her* that way, Margo promised herself.

"Are you having a good time?" Lila asked. "I was kind of worried. You weren't exactly the life of the party at my house this afternoon. . . . Oh, Tony, this is one of my favorite songs. We've got to dance to this one. See you after this dance, Jess—"

"Bye," Margo said with a wave. This was great, she thought. Both Lila and Todd had instantly recognized her as one of the Wakefield twins. Okay, so they had thought she was Jessica, not Elizabeth. But that was a minor point. It wouldn't be long now before she had her Elizabeth act down perfectly, and then . . .

"Hey, Jess!" called Steven Wakefield, strolling over with an arm around a pretty girl. Both of them were wearing large, black mouse ears. "Great costume, little sis," he said, swatting her playfully on the backside as he walked on.

"I can't believe I'm wearing this thing in public, Jessica," Amy Sutton complained, joining her a minute later. "I'm not supposed to tell, but I can't stand it anymore. I lost a bet with Winston."

Ahhh, thought Margo. The skinny kid with the thick glasses and the screaming brat of a baby . . .

The baby Elizabeth loves, said the voice in her head. *The baby who doesn't deserve so much good luck, when other babies had nobody at all to love them.*

"Well, you know Winston," Margo said in response to Amy's comment.

Amy nodded. "Unfortunately."

"Hi, Jessica!" called a girl whose name Margo didn't know. She smiled broadly as the girl walked on.

It was wonderful to be so popular. Margo couldn't remember when she'd had a better time.

"Yo, Wakefield!" called one of the best-looking guys in the place. He was dressed as a sultan.

"Isn't it about time for you to turn into a pumpkin?" Bruce asked Margo loudly, from across the dance floor.

"Looks like you beat me to it!" Margo called back, pointing to his orange robes.

"Good one, Jessica!" yelled another handsome boy she didn't recognize.

This is fabulous! Jessica Wakefield knew every good-looking guy in town. For the first time in her life, Margo felt as if she really belonged.

"Glad to see you're feeling better, Jessica!" said a tall girl who was dressed as a witch.

"Have you heard who the judges have picked for the costume contest?" Amy asked.

"No," Margo said. "I didn't think they'd announced the winners yet."

"They haven't," Amy explained. "But I heard a rumor that Steven and Billie are going to win in the category for Best Couple!"

"That's great!" Margo said, genuinely pleased. A lot of things were great, Margo thought. She was one of the most popular girls in town, from one of the most popular families in town. And everybody here loved her. Everybody—

Suddenly, Margo spotted a disturbingly familiar face.

"No," Margo said under her breath. *Not now. Not when everything is so perfect.* But Josh hadn't seen her yet. Margo still had time to get away.

"I'll catch you later, Amy," she said quickly. "I'm, uh, going to look for James."

Josh scanned the crowd one last time, almost ready to call it quits for the night. He had been at the costume party for hours, slipping around the clusters of cheerful, excited, innocent people, as he searched for one who was not so innocent.

Had his instincts been wrong? Perhaps Margo hadn't come to the party tonight. Perhaps she sensed he would be there, and had stayed away.

Just then something registered in the corner

of Josh's eye. A girl wearing a pink, frothy-looking gown seemed to be hurrying away from him. She looked about five-foot-six, and slim. A pink veil cascaded gently back over her blond hair.

Was it Margo?

He began dodging through the crowded garden in pursuit. At one point, the girl turned to duck under an arch, and Josh caught sight of her face, pale between large earrings that flashed like stars. It *was* Margo. The golden hair was wrong, of course, but she'd been a blonde when he'd spotted her in the parking lot of Valley Mall, too. It had to be a wig, or a dye job.

Josh was running now. His weeks of searching were about to pay off. He skirted a tall boxwood hedge and dashed through the latticework arch, into a small courtyard with a fountain in the middle of it. He stood just inside the archway, panting, as he stared around the flagstone patio. The courtyard was empty.

He stomped back through the archway into the main part of the garden. Then he began scanning the party guests once more, not really expecting to see her.

Miraculously, she was there. About thirty feet away from him, past the refreshments table, Margo stood by herself in the pale pink princess costume. She was gazing toward the dance floor and didn't even seem to notice Josh.

Josh marveled at Margo's composure. She had even more nerve than he had realized. Perhaps Margo knew exactly what she was doing, and was tracking him carefully out of the corner of her eye.

Josh shook his head and began stepping toward Margo slowly and deliberately, keeping an eye on her profile.

He waited until he was only a few feet away from Margo, then he sprang, grabbing her roughly around the shoulders.

The girl screamed and began to struggle, but Josh knew that he was physically stronger than Margo—and that her movements were hampered by her heavy ball gown. He held her firmly around the shoulders, ignoring the pain of her high heels stabbing him in the legs as she kicked him.

"What are you doing?" demanded an angry voice. A tall boy about Josh's age, appeared out of nowhere, wearing a blue tunic and a makeshift crown.

"I'm all right, James," the girl replied breathlessly. "Get away from me!" she screamed at Josh, elbowing him in the side.

James grabbed Josh from behind and tried to pull him off of the girl. Then Josh fell, stunned, from a sudden blow to the side of his head. He looked up to see a skinny boy of about sixteen wielding a set of bongo drums.

James pulled Josh up from the ground and held him securely.

"Are you okay, Jessica?" the skinny boy asked, helping her up from where she had fallen when Josh went sprawling. "Who is this creep, anyway?"

"I'm fine." The girl nodded. "Thanks, guys. I don't know who he is. I've never seen him before."

"Her name is Margo. . . ." Josh began weakly.

"My name is Jessica!" declared the girl Josh had grabbed.

Josh was utterly confused. Somehow, he had grabbed the wrong girl. He looked back and forth among the hostile faces surrounding him.

"I think I've made a terrible mistake," he began, haltingly. He scrutinized the girl's face. *How could anyone look so much like Margo and not be Margo?*

"You certainly have made a mistake," James said, still gripping his arms from behind.

"What's going on here?" said another female voice, this one full of concern. "Jessica?" she asked uncertainly.

Josh turned to face the newcomers, and

felt the color drain from his face.

It was Margo. Again.

Josh blinked his eyes quickly. He was seeing things. It was the only explanation. Here was a second girl in a full pink ball gown, with a shawl that shimmered like moonlight and a filmy veil floating like mist on her blond hair.

"This is impossible. . . ." he began in a whisper. "I'm sorry," he said to Jessica, barely able to choke out the words. "I thought you were someone else."

Harry, who had run over when he'd heard all the commotion, began lecturing him on how to act at other people's houses, but Josh could see nothing but the twin princesses in pink gowns.

"Here's your shawl, Jess," Amy said, handing it to her. "And I found one of your pearl earrings on the ground, too."

As Jessica took the pearl earring, Josh noticed that her mirror image wore smaller, shinier earrings.

"Do you want to press charges, Jessica?" Harry asked.

Jessica shook her head. "No," she said quickly. "I'm not hurt. Let's just forget it ever happened."

"Yes, let's forget it," said Elizabeth. "Let's get out of here," she said, taking a boy's arm.

Harry unceremoniously escorted Josh out of the garden and practically booted him into the street.

Josh didn't argue. As he walked away from the mansion, he replayed the events of the last half hour in his mind, trying to make sense of it all. He had finally found Margo. In fact, he had found two of her. But neither one was her. It didn't make any sense.

Perhaps he had found the real Margo as well, Josh told himself. The girl he first spotted near the dance floor had run from him. So she had to be Margo—didn't she?

Josh's mind was going in circles. He tried to remember every detail of the last time he'd seen that first Margo. She had stopped at the small, latticework archway that led to the little courtyard with the fountain. Her face had been pale, and her earrings had flashed like stars as she spun around and disappeared through the arch.

Josh stopped walking, focusing on the memory of that sparkle of jewels on either side of her face. *The first Margo wore large, rhinestone earrings!*

"That was the real Margo," Josh said, convinced.

It was an incredible coincidence that Margo would travel thousands of miles and come across the very town where her two look-alikes lived. What if it wasn't a coincidence? What if it was all part of some psychotic plan of Margo's? Could Margo be planning to somehow make use of the fact that Jessica and Elizabeth looked exactly like her?

Josh felt his knees turn to jelly at the implications that were swimming through his brain. He wasn't sure of exactly what Margo was scheming, but one thing was certain—the twins Jessica and Elizabeth were in terrible danger.

Chapter 11

Winston had just finished changing Daisy's diaper late the next morning when the doorbell rang. He lifted the baby in his arms and scrambled toward the door, nearly tripping over the bag with the dancing hippopotamuses on it.

"Hi, Winston!" said the girl from the day-care center when he opened the door. "Sorry to barge in on you like this, but I wanted to talk to you about Daisy."

Winston was taken aback. He didn't remember having given this girl his address.

"Can I come in?" she asked.

Winston stepped aside to let her pass, and then followed her into the living room, neatly sidestepping the hippopotamus bag.

"Uh, what can I do for you?" Winston asked

as he motioned her to sit on the couch.

As he did, he glanced around the room as someone might who was seeing it for the first time. A week ago, the sofa had been off-white. Now, it was a lot farther off. The white carpeting looked more like beige, and was littered with baby toys, the wet diaper he'd just removed, a pizza box, and the remains of Winston's last peanut-butter-and-sardine sandwich.

His heart sank as he remembered a sobering reality—his parents would be home that very night. He sat on the other end of the couch, holding Daisy securely against his shoulder.

"Winston, it's time to face the fact that Daisy's parents have abandoned her."

"How could they do such a thing?" Winston asked, almost in a wail.

"I don't know," the girl said. Then her eyes grew very cold and she said in a completely expressionless voice, "A lot of people do terrible things to children."

Winston shivered.

"Look, Winston. I know how difficult this is for you," she continued. "I can make it easier," she said. "I'll take Daisy to Social Services for you. The Project Youth center has a liaison in that office. We'll take care of everything for you. That way, you won't have to hand her over to strangers."

Winston knew that the girl was right. It was time for him to face facts.

He looked her straight in the eyes and was about to agree to her proposal, but something stopped him.

"No," he said suddenly, surprising himself. "My parents will be back in town tonight. I think I'll wait until then before I take any action."

For an instant, he thought he caught a flash of anger in the curly-haired girl's eyes, but it was gone before he was sure that he had even seen it.

"All right, Winston," she said, a little too loudly. "If that's the way you want to play it, we'll give it a few more days. But you look as if you've been running yourself ragged. I bet you've hardly let Daisy out of your sight in a week. You've been so busy taking care of her that you probably haven't gotten a single other thing accomplished in days. Am I right?"

"Well—"

"That settles it," she said. "Go out now, get your shopping done, pick up your dry cleaning, visit a friend, or whatever. I'll stay here and take care of Daisy for a couple of hours, free of charge."

"I don't think so—"

"Winston, I am a professional day-care

193

provider," she reminded him. "I'm not some psycho baby-killer."

"All right," Winston said. He was a little uncertain, but he couldn't think of a single reason why he shouldn't take advantage of the offer. "If I don't get to the grocery store soon, Daisy and I will be eating her pacifier for dinner tonight. And it's time for her nap, so she's not likely to give you any trouble. I had her out kind of late last night, so she's pretty tired."

Winston felt a stab of fear as he handed the baby over to the curly-haired girl with the oddly vacant eyes. But she cooed and cuddled Daisy as gently as Maria or Elizabeth would have, and he told himself that he was being paranoid.

As Winston prepared to leave the house a few minutes later, he bent over to kiss Daisy on the forehead. "Bye bye, rug rat!" he said. "You take a nice, long nap for your new baby-sitter."

Daisy smiled prettily and, with Margo's help, waved her tiny hand at him.

"Goo-boo," she called.

"I thought that dorky Egbert character would never leave!" Margo exclaimed as the door shut behind Winston.

Margo held the baby up so that she was looking straight into Daisy's face. "This is the first step," she told the child in a cold, expressionless voice. "Elizabeth loves you—but now you're mine to control."

Daisy stared at her quizzically, cocking her head.

"I know you're not as dumb as you act," Margo said to the baby.

Daisy began to whimper.

"If there's one thing I can't stand, it's sniveling babies," Margo said. "It's time for you to take a nap and stop bothering me."

She shoved the baby under her arm, like a football, and carried her upstairs.

Daisy was crying in earnest now. Margo raised her voice to be heard above the baby's wails. "Which room is it, brat?" she asked.

Margo pushed open the nearest door. It was obviously a boy's room, but a large, white crib dominated it.

Margo dumped the baby onto her back in the crib. "There!" she said coldly. "Now stop making all that blasted noise!"

Margo bolted from the room, leaving the baby alone in the semidarkness. Daisy kept right on crying.

A minute later, Margo was back. "You were supposed to shut up when I put you in bed, you little brat," she said, pounding her fists repeatedly against the side of the crib.

With every wail, Daisy's face became redder. Margo laughed derisively at the way her weak little hands flailed in the air.

"You thought you were going to have it all," she said, glaring down at her. "You thought you would have all these popular people caring about you. But that's not the way it happens when your parents leave you. It didn't happen that way for me, and it's not going to happen that way for you. I'll make sure of it."

Daisy's wails turned to screams.

"Don't you dare do this to me!" Margo demanded, raising her voice. "Stop that noise now!"

Margo closed her eyes as one of her pounding headaches overwhelmed her. She grabbed the pillow from Winston's bed, and, shoving it against Daisy's twisted little face, instantly muffled the baby's desperate cries. Margo smiled.

At that instant, the doorbell rang.

Margo's eyes widened. Whoever it was must have heard the baby's cries.

Margo pounded a fist against the side of the crib, then ran out of the room and down the stairs, pursued by the sounds of Daisy's strengthening howls.

When Margo opened the front door, she felt the color drain from her face. Elizabeth

Wakefield stood directly in front of her.

"I, um, was just coming over to see if I could take care of the baby for Winston for a while," Elizabeth said haltingly, glancing past Margo toward the sound of Daisy's screams.

For weeks, Margo had been preparing for the day when she would stand face-to-face with Elizabeth Wakefield. But she hadn't expected it here, so soon. For the first time in her life, Margo was speechless. She slipped past Elizabeth and bolted out of the house.

Elizabeth stood in the doorway for an instant, uncertain about whether she should pursue the unsettling girl who had just run from Winston's house. But Daisy's heartrending screams made up her mind for her. She rushed inside and leaped up the stairs two at a time.

A minute later, she stood in Winston's room, holding Daisy in her arms.

"There, there, sweetheart," Elizabeth murmured soothingly. "Don't cry. Everything's going to be all right."

As Daisy's screams quieted to whimpers, Elizabeth admitted to herself that the baby wasn't the only one who needed comforting. Elizabeth was still trembling from her meeting with the strange, curly-haired girl at the door.

Where had she seen her before?

For some reason, Elizabeth suddenly remembered the sweet smell of flowers in the private courtyard of Harry Minton's garden. In her mind, she saw her sister materializing in the arched entrance—like pink mist in the black, star-studded night—before dissolving silently into the surrounding darkness.

Out of the darkness, an image from Elizabeth's recurring nightmare engulfed her in a cold wave of fear, just as it had in the small courtyard the night before. Her sister's blank, blue eyes stared at her wordlessly. In her hand, the brittle sunlight glinted off the surface of the cruel knife.

Elizabeth gasped and held the baby closer. The girl at Winston's door had the same blue eyes.

Elizabeth sat on the edge of Winston's bed, watching Daisy as she fell asleep. The doorbell rang, and Elizabeth jumped. For an instant, she was afraid that the curly-haired girl had returned. Then she shook her head, dismissing the thought.

The doorbell rang again, and Elizabeth rose. Daisy stirred, so Elizabeth lifted her gently and carried her downstairs.

Maria Santelli was at the door, holding a bag of groceries.

"Elizabeth," she said, walking in. "I didn't expect to see you here. I ran into Winston downtown, and he told me he left the baby here with a sitter. Where'd she go?"

Elizabeth opened her mouth to tell Maria everything, but she stopped herself. She didn't know for sure that the curly-haired girl had done anything wrong. She would tell Winston, certainly, but it wouldn't be right for her to spread rumors that could hurt somebody's reputation.

"I, uh, dropped by a half hour ago to see if Winston needed any help with the baby," she explained. "Daisy didn't need two of us, so the baby-sitter, um, left."

Maria jiggled the baby's foot and gave her a peck on the forehead.

"When do you expect Winston back?" Elizabeth asked, trying not to sound anxious.

"He should be here in half an hour or so," Maria said, shoving a stack of dirty dishes out of the way to clear a place on the counter for her grocery bag. "I told him I'd send the sitter home and start something to eat. I can watch Daisy while I fix lunch. There's no need for you to hang around, too."

Elizabeth looked at her uncertainly. "I really

need to talk to Winston," she said. "Maybe I should wait."

"You can stay if you want to," Maria said, pulling a package of tortellini from the grocery bag. "In fact, you're welcome to have lunch with us—pasta salad. Or I can tell Winston to give you a call when he gets in."

Maria opened a cupboard and selected a serving bowl, before turning back to Elizabeth. "Are you all right, Liz? You seem a little nervous."

Elizabeth smiled weakly. "Oh, I'm fine. I'm just kind of tired," she said. She looked down at the yawning baby in her arms. "Daisy's not the only who stayed out late last night! I'll just put her back in her crib, and then I'll get going. But, Maria, please tell Win to give me a call when he comes home."

"Are you sure you can handle it all by yourself?" Maria asked Winston as she hung the damp dishrag around the faucet and dried her hands on her jeans.

"Piece of cake," Winston said, drying the last dish and stacking it with all the others. "We've now washed and dried every plate, bowl, and kitchen utensil the Egbert family owns—after spending the week setting a record for dirtying them. All I have to do before my parents get home is call in the National Guard for disaster-relief services in the living room, rent a bull-dozer to clear away the baby toys in my bedroom, and hire a wrecking ball to demolish the whole house so we can start fresh. As I said, piece of cake."

Maria laughed. "I'll take your word for it. Did you have a chance to call Liz? She really wanted to talk to you. She seemed upset."

"Not yet," Winston admitted, "but I will."

He trudged into the living room and sat down on the couch with a sigh. Maria sat beside him. "What's wrong, Winston? Is it Liz?"

"Not exactly, but I think I know what she wants to talk to me about. And I know she's right. I can't go on like this. I'm going to have to give Daisy to someone official. I guess her parents aren't coming back."

Maria put her hand on his arm. "I think you're right," she said quietly. "But I know how tough it is for you. Do you want me to come down to Social Services with you?"

Winston shook his head. "No," he said. "A worker at the Project Youth day-care center said she'd take Daisy to the right people. I just have to get Daisy out of bed, collect her stuff, and drive her down there. And I feel like I should do it myself."

Maria nodded. "I understand. You want to say good-bye to her. Actually, I'd like to say good-bye, too. I'll get her up from her nap and change her, while you start packing up all her things. Then you can take her to the day-care center."

"Thanks," Winston said. He sighed heavily, stood up, and walked over to the entrance foyer, where the hippopotamus tote bag still sat in the center of the floor. He reached down to pick it up by its handles, realizing that he was actually going to miss it.

Winston sat in his orange Volkswagen bug, staring forlornly at the front window of Little Darlings Day Care.

He unlatched his seat belt, climbed out of the car, and circled it, feeling as if he were walking toward a firing squad. He opened the right-side door and slid into the backseat beside Daisy's car seat.

"Hi there, rug rat. How's Uncle Winston's little girl?"

Daisy smiled broadly. "Dah-dah!"

Winston shook his head. "No, not Dah-dah. Win-ston. Can Daisy say 'Winston'?"

"Dah-dah!"

Winston wiped a tear from his face. "Okay,"

he said, biting his bottom lip. "I give up. You can call me Dah-dah if you want to."

Daisy smiled, showing her tiny white tooth. Winston unbuckled the straps of the car seat, lifted the baby out of it, and held her against his chest.

"I'm going to miss you, rug rat," he whispered, kissing her on the cheek.

He backed out of the car and held her securely in one arm while he reached back in to grab the hippopotamus bag. Then he took a deep breath and walked slowly but resolutely into the day-care center.

"Well, I guess that's about it," Winston said to the day-care girl. "I've written down her parents' name and address for you. Everything you'll need is in the bag."

The baby-sitter smiled and held out her hands to take the baby, but her turquoise eyes still looked cold and blank to Winston. He kept Daisy against his shoulder, bouncing her gently the way she liked it.

Winston looked at the curly-haired girl and felt a shudder pass through his body. But he was sure that his doubts were unfounded. After all, she was a trained professional. He would probably be reluctant to leave Daisy with anyone who was a stranger.

"I guess that's it," he said again.

"Except the baby," the girl prompted.

"Be careful with her," Winston said. "She can creep along on the floor pretty fast, if you don't watch her carefully, and she sleeps—"

The girl interrupted. "Don't worry, Winston. You can be sure I'll give her the kind of care she deserves. Besides, my shift here is over in a few minutes. I'll bring her over to Social Services right away."

Winston took a deep breath and held Daisy out in front of himself so that he could take one last look at her. He kissed Daisy gently on the forehead, then handed her to the girl with the curly brown hair and walked to the door.

Winston hadn't planned to look back, but he couldn't help himself. He turned and gave Daisy one last, watery smile. She grinned back, delighted.

"Goo-boo," Winston said to her. Then he walked out the door, leaving Daisy in the hands of the baby-sitter.

As he left, it occurred to Winston that the girl had never told him her name.

Chapter 12

Winston saw a strange car in the driveway as he stopped the Volkswagen in front of his house. His eyes widened. A plump, dark-haired woman was standing on his front doorstep, ringing the bell. It was Betsy Zvonchenko, Daisy's mother.

Winston jumped out of the Volkswagen and sprinted to the front door.

"Oh, Winston!" Mrs. Zvonchenko began. "I'm so glad you're home. I apologize for having been away for a whole week. Your poor mother must have been frantic, with the baby to take care of all that time, and not knowing where I was. I suppose she must be out now. Is Daisy with her?"

Winston opened his mouth to reply, but the woman went right on talking.

"I'm so sorry, Winston. You know how those

205

little Central American countries are. I brought Ian's birth certificate all the way down there, but then we still couldn't get through customs because of some mix-up with the paperwork. Communication with the outside world was down, because of the coup, so I couldn't even call to let you know we'd been delayed."

"Mrs. Zvon—" Winston interrupted desperately.

"I don't know what you must think of me," the woman continued. "Well, they finally let Ian go—that's him in the car, you know. And here we are—"

"And Daisy's not!" Winston broke in. "We've got to go get her before the baby-sitter turns her over to Social Services."

Mrs. Zvonchenko's eyes widened, and for once she was speechless. Winston grabbed her arm, dragged her to her dark-blue Oldsmobile, and jumped into the backseat himself. "I'll explain on the way and give you directions," he said, ignoring Ian Zvonchenko's startled stare. "Drive fast!" he ordered.

The Oldsmobile careened out of the driveway, throwing Winston against the seat back, and he realized that they might actually make it to the day-care center before the curly-haired employee took Daisy to Social Services.

Fortunately, Mrs. Zvonchenko could drive as fast as she could talk.

"This is is the place!" he yelped as the car pulled in front of Little Darlings. Winston was out of the car and running toward the front door before the Oldsmobile had stopped.

He threw open the door, ran past a roomful of surprised four-year-olds, and skidded to a stop at the door of the room where he'd left Daisy with the curly-haired girl.

From inside the room, Winston could hear a baby's desperate screams, but he couldn't be sure that it was Daisy. After all, this was a day-care center. The place was crawling with kids. The baby's cries were quickly muffled at the same instant as he grabbed the doorknob and tried to turn it. The door was locked.

"It's Winston Egbert!" he called frantically, pounding his fists against the wooden door. "Is Daisy still here? Her parents came back!"

The Zvonchenkos hurried in and stood behind Winston, both of them wringing their hands.

A minute later, the door opened and the curly-haired girl emerged from the room, looking more flustered than Winston had ever seen her.

"Is Daisy still here?" he asked again.

207

Something that looked like anger flashed icily in her blue eyes, but it was gone in an instant. "She's here," the girl said in a monotone. She opened the door wider and Winston rushed in to find Daisy lying on her back on a table, next to a large pillow. Daisy's face was pink and she was whimpering, but she smiled broadly when Winston picked her up.

"Ba-wooo!" she said, her pearl-like tooth showing.

"Baba-looo!" Winston replied, hugging her. When he handed Daisy to her mother, the little girl seemed reluctant to let go of him.

"Goo-boo, rug rat," he said to Daisy as she reached for him over her mother's shoulder. Winston hoped that nobody could see the tears in his eyes.

"Goo-boo," Daisy repeated obediently. "Ba-woooo!"

Winston followed the Zvonchenkos out of the room, happily swinging the hippopotamus bag by his side. *All's well that ends well*, he thought. Daisy would go home with her parents, Winston would be a carefree kid again, and the authorities would never have to know a thing about the past week—if the day-care girl agreed not to say anything.

Winston turned to speak to her, but the room

was empty. The baby-sitter was gone.

Margo sat cross-legged on her bed, thumbing through the pages of a phone book she had stolen from her landlady.

"Rats!" she said loudly, for the fifth time since she'd been home that day. Twice today, she'd almost been caught—first by Elizabeth and then by Winston. Not to mention that close brush with Josh Smith at the party last night.

"If I'm not more careful, I could still blow this whole thing!" she said. Then her voice lapsed into a low, raspy sound. *"Beware overconfidence."* The voice in Margo's head used to come only silently, echoing in her mind. Lately, it had begun speaking through her mouth as well. She was becoming one with the voice. She was the voice.

She stared at a page of the phone book, but her cold, blue eyes were turned inward. In her mind's eye, Margo saw flames of orange fire leaping into the night sky. She heard the frightened calls of her little foster sister, trapped in the burning house. Margo smiled, pushing her fear behind her. She had carried out that plan. She would succeed with this one, even if she had lost her chance with Daisy.

"Time's running out," she said resolutely. "It's

sooner than I'd planned, but it's too risky to wait. It's time to move this plan into its final phase."

Her finger scanned the listings for lawyers. "Ned Wakefield, attorney at law," she read aloud. "All I need is Dear Old Dad's business address, and then I'll be ready for the grand finale."

Margo knew she would learn to love Ned Wakefield. He was the perfect father. Okay, maybe he was a little square, but he was good-looking and well-respected, he wasn't a drunk, and he would never hurt anyone. She occasionally felt a twinge of jealousy toward him, but she was sure she would overcome it in time. It was easy to be jealous of someone that Alice Wakefield was in love with. But Margo knew she couldn't have her mother all to herself. At least not yet.

For now, it was enough to be part of a perfect family. If others started getting too possessive of her mother, well, she might have to come up with a plan to deal with the problem.

Margo scurried to her typewriter. She cheerfully typed Mr. Wakefield's business address, hunting and pecking her way through the keys. Elizabeth could type, so Margo knew she had better learn, too. It was taking longer than she expected, but that was all right. There would be plenty of time to perfect her technique later, while working on articles for the school newspaper.

As she typed, Margo read occasional snatches of her work aloud. "Have followed your career with enthusiasm . . . impressed by your integrity during the recent mayoral race . . . consulting contract that could prove quite interesting . . . Fairmont Hotel . . ."

When she was finished with the letter, Margo slowly licked the envelope, savoring it as if it were a stick of candy. She would personally drop it by Ned Wakefield's law office the next morning; the mail would take too long.

Margo gazed intently at the name on the outside of the envelope. "Have a lovely trip," she said darkly. "When you get home, you'll have a new daughter."

Jessica looked across the dining-room table at her sister on Monday night, her expression forlorn. Elizabeth wouldn't even glance at her.

At the party Saturday, when her twin came running to her aid after Sherlock Holmes had tried to attack her, Jessica had felt a spark of hope for their relationship. Elizabeth had been genuinely concerned. Jessica heard it in her voice; she had seen the fear and love in her sister's eyes. But Elizabeth had backed away as soon as she'd seen that Jessica was unhurt.

Jessica sighed. Maybe her mother was right. Maybe Elizabeth's coldness would eventually thaw. Maybe in time, she'd be able to admit that she still cared about Jessica.

"Hey, clones!" Steven said, breezing into the room.

"Are you still here?" Elizabeth asked.

"Don't fall all over each other, telling me how glad you are to have me home," he teased.

Elizabeth smiled warmly, and Jessica felt a twinge of envy. "Sorry, Steve," Elizabeth said. "I didn't mean it like that. I thought you had gone back to school."

"I decided I could use one more home-cooked meal before I went back to dorm food," Steve explained. He raised his voice to call into the kitchen. "Need any help, Mom?"

"No," Alice Wakefield responded, walking into the dining room with a basket of bread in her hands. "Jessica did most of the cooking tonight. I'm just serving it."

Steven looked at Jessica and raised his eyebrows in a gesture that conveyed both mock surprise and real concern. She supposed she looked as miserable as she felt. But she ignored Steven. If she felt like helping with dinner now and then, why should everyone make a federal case out of it? They were the ones who were always complaining that she didn't do enough work around the house.

Alice laid the basket of bread on the table. Then she untied the apron that covered her stylish red suit and stood with her hands on her hips. "I don't know where your father is," she said. "He called half an hour ago and said he was on his way home, with exciting news."

"And here he is," came Ned Wakefield's voice. He strode into the room, depositing his briefcase on a chair near the door. "Dinner looks great," he said, sitting down.

"Don't get your hopes up," Steven warned. "Jessica made it." He looked toward her, obviously expecting a retort. Jessica silently passed him the bread.

"I received an interesting letter today," their father began, not noticing the awkward moment, "from a woman named Michelle de Voice. She's in the legal department of an environmental engineering firm in San Francisco. Her company followed the events here in Sweet Valley a few months back, during the election for mayor. She says she was impressed by my part in restoring Peter Santelli's candidacy and stopping the developer from destroying the coastline to turn

Sweet Valley into a commercial venture."

He reached for the salad and served himself, eyeing his family to see if they were in suspense.

"The crux of it is that she wants to talk with me about a consulting contract with her firm. The letter doesn't have a lot of details, but it could be interesting." He paused dramatically. "It also could mean a lot of money."

"It sounds wonderful, honey," Alice said, passing the quiche to Elizabeth. "What's the next step?"

"She wants to meet with me next Monday. She's reserved a room—at the Fairmont Hotel— and has invited *the two of us* to drive up for an interview and dinner. She's even been kind enough to get us the room for two nights, so that we don't have to rush through it all. Can you arrange to play hooky from work?"

"I'm sure I can manage it," Alice said. "Will you two girls be all right alone here for two nights?"

"Of course, Mom," Elizabeth replied, smiling, trying to hide the sudden uneasiness she felt. "We'll be perfectly safe."

"Perfectly safe," Jessica echoed, but as she did, she looked across the table into her sister's blue eyes and saw the apprehension mirrored there. A shiver ran down her spine.

Collect all the books in the Sweet Valley High series,
now over 100 titles strong!

Ask your bookseller for these Sweet Valley
Supers and Magnas.

SUPER EDITIONS:
- PERFECT SUMMER
- SPECIAL CHRISTMAS
- SPRING BREAK
- MALIBU SUMMER
- WINTER CARNIVAL
- SPRING FEVER

SUPER THRILLERS:
- DOUBLE JEOPARDY
- ON THE RUN
- NO PLACE TO HIDE
- DEADLY SUMMER
- MURDER ON THE LINE
- BEWARE THE WOLFMAN

SUPER STARS:
- LILA'S STORY
- BRUCE'S STORY
- ENID'S STORY
- OLIVIA'S STORY
- TODD'S STORY

MAGNA EDITIONS:
- THE WAKEFIELDS OF
  SWEET VALLEY
- THE WAKEFIELD LEGACY:
  THE UNTOLD STORY
- A NIGHT TO REMEMBER

And don't miss this sensational six-part miniseries—
Sweet Valley will never be the same!

#95	THE MORNING AFTER
#96	THE ARREST
#97	THE VERDICT
#98	THE WEDDING
#99	BEWARE THE BABY-SITTER
#100	THE EVIL TWIN (MAGNA)

Life after high school gets even sweeter!

Jessica and Elizabeth are now freshman at Sweet Valley University, where the motto is: Welcome to college – welcome to freedom!

Don't miss any of the books in this fabulous new series.

♡ College Girls #1 ....56308-4 $3.50/4.50 Can.
♡ Love, Lies and Jessica Wakefield #2........56306-8 $3.50/4.50 Can.

- -

Your friends at Sweet Valley High have had their world turned upside down!

Meet one person with a power so evil, so dangerous, that it could destroy the entire world of Sweet Valley!

A Night to Remember, the book that starts it all, is followed by a six book series filled with romance, drama and suspense.

29309-5 A NIGHT TO REMEMBER (Magna Edition) ..$3.99/4.99 Can.
29852-6 THE MORNING AFTER #95 ....$3.50/4.50 Can.
29853-4 THE ARREST #96 ....$3.50/4.50 Can.
29854-2 THE VERDICT #97 ....$3.50/4.50 Can.
29855-0 THE WEDDING #98 ....$3.50/4.50 Can.
29856-9 BEWARE THE BABYSITTER #99 ....$3.50/4.50 Can.
29857-7 THE EVIL TWIN #100 ....$3.99/4.99 Can.

Life after high school gets even *Sweeter!*

Jessica and Elizabeth are now freshmen at Sweet Valley University, where the motto is: Welcome to college — welcome to freedom!

Don't miss any of the books in this fabulous new series.

SIGN UP FOR THE SWEET VALLEY HIGH® FAN CLUB!

Hey, girls! Get all the gossip on Sweet Valley High's® most popular teenagers when you join our fantastic Fan Club! As a member, you'll get all of this really cool stuff:

- Membership Card with your own personal Fan Club ID number
- A Sweet Valley High® Secret Treasure Box
- Sweet Valley High® Stationery
- Official Fan Club Pencil (for secret note writing!)
- Three Bookmarks
- A "Members Only" Door Hanger
- Two Skeins of J. & P. Coats® Embroidery Floss with flower barrette instruction leaflet
- Two editions of *The Oracle* newsletter
- Plus exclusive Sweet Valley High® product offers, special savings, contests, and much more!

Be the first to find out what Jessica & Elizabeth Wakefield are up to by joining the Sweet Valley High® Fan Club for the one-year membership fee of only $6.25 each for U.S. residents, $8.25 for Canadian residents (U.S. currency). Includes shipping & handling.

Send a check or money order (do not send cash) made payable to "Sweet Valley High® Fan Club" along with this form to:

SWEET VALLEY HIGH® FAN CLUB, BOX 3919-B, SCHAUMBURG, IL 60168-3919

NAME_____
                        (Please print clearly)

ADDRESS_____

CITY_____ STATE _____ ZIP_____
                                                                (Required)

AGE _____ BIRTHDAY_____ /_____ /_____

Offer good while supplies last. Allow 6-8 weeks after check clearance for delivery. Addresses without ZIP codes cannot be honored. Offer good in USA & Canada only. Void where prohibited by law.
©1993 by Francine Pascal   LCI-1383-193